REYNOLDS PRICE

"A wonderful, compelling storyteller with a keen sense of time and place."

Houston Chronicle

"Reynolds Price is a sensitive witness to the full range of humanity. He shows people as they truly are, not as they picture themselves."

The Grand Rapids Press

"One of our most gifted writers."

Publishers Weekly

"Reynolds Price, like Faulkner before him, is a powerful writer and an excellent craftsman."

Chicago Tribune

"A fine storyteller."

Library Journal

THE NAMES AND FACES OF HEROES

Reynolds Price

BALLANTINE BOOKS • NEW YORK

These stories have appeared, some in different forms, in THE ARCHIVE, COUNTRY BEAUTIFUL, DUKE UNIVERSITY ALUMNI REGISTER, SHENANDOAH, THE VIRGINIA QUARTERLY REVIEW *and an anthology,* WINTER'S TALES

Library of Congress Catalog Card Number: 63-12414

ISBN 0-345-36182-2

This edition published by arrangement with Atheneum Publishers, an imprint of Macmillan Publishing Company.

Manufactured in the United States of America

First Ballantine Books Edition: November 1989

CONTENTS

I met a plow on my first going out at my gate the first morning after my arrival, & the Plowboy said to the Plowman, "Father, The Gate is Open."

WILLIAM BLAKE *to* THOMAS BUTTS,
23 September 1800

A CHAIN OF LOVE

THEY HAD OBSERVED PAPA'S BIRTHDAY WITH A freezer of cream even if it was the dead of winter, and they had given him a Morris chair that was not brand new but was what he had always wanted. The next morning he was sick, and nobody could figure the connection between such nice hand-turned cream that Rato almost froze to death making and a tired heart which was what he had according to Dr. Sledge. Papa said "Tired of what?" and refused to go to any hospital. He said he would die at home if it was his time, but the family saw it different so they took him to Raleigh in Milo's car—pulled out the backseat that hadn't been out since Milo married the Abbott girl and spread a pallet and laid him there on pillows with his head resting on the hand-painted one off the settee, the gray felt pillow from Natural Bridge, Virginia that he brought Pauline his wife six years be-

1

fore she died, off that two-day excursion he took with
the County Agent to the model peanut farms around
Suffolk.

Much as she wanted to, Mama couldn't stay with
Papa then. (Mama was his daughter-in-law.) She made
him a half a gallon of boiled custard as he asked her to,
to take along, and she rode down to Raleigh with
them, but she had to come back with Milo in the evening. It worried her not being able to stay when staying was her duty, but they were having a Children's
Day at the church that coming Sunday—mainly because the Christmas pageant had fallen through when
John Arthur Bobbitt passed around German measles
like a dish of cool figs at the first rehearsal—and since
she had organized the Sunbeams single-handed, she
couldn't leave them then right on the verge of public
performance. So they took Rosacoke and Rato along
to sit for the first days till Mama could come back herself. Dr. Sledge said there was no need to take on a
full-time nurse with two strong grandchildren dying to
sit with him anyhow.

And there wasn't. From the minute Papa had his
attack, there was never a question of Rosacoke going
if Papa had to go—no question of *wanting* to go—and
in fact she almost liked the idea. There was just one
thing made her think twice about it, which was missing
one Saturday night with Wesley. Wesley Beavers was
Rosacoke's boyfriend even if Mama didn't like the
idea of her riding in to town with a boy two years older
every Saturday night to the show and sitting with him
afterwards in his car—Rato there on the porch in the
pitch dark looking—and telling him goodbye without
a word. That was the best part of any week, telling

Wesley goodbye the way she did when he pulled his Pontiac up in the yard under the pecan tree, and if it was fall, nuts would hit the car every now and then like enemy bullets to make them laugh or if it was spring, all those little rain frogs would be singing-out over behind the creek and then for a minute calming as if they had all died together or had just stopped to catch their breath. But Wesley would be there when she got back, and anyhow going to the hospital would give her a chance to lay out of school for a week, and it would give her extra time with Papa that she liked to be with. Rosacoke's Papa was her grandfather. Her own father was dead, run over by a green pick-up truck one Saturday evening late a long time ago, almost before she could remember.

But Rato could remember. Rato had seen a lot of things die. He was named for their father—Horatio Junior Mustian—and he was the next-to-oldest boy, nearly eighteen. He didn't mind staying with Papa either. He didn't go to school, hadn't gone in four years, so he didn't have the pleasure of laying out the way Rosacoke did, but seeing all the people would be enough for Rato. Not that he liked people so much. You could hardly get him to speak to anybody, but if you left him alone he would take what pleasure he needed, just standing there taller than anybody else and thinner and watching them.

Dr. Sledge had called on ahead, and they didn't have any trouble getting Papa in the hospital. He even had the refusal of a big corner room with a private bath, but it cost twelve dollars a day. Papa said there was no use trying the good will of Blue Cross Hospital Insurance so he took a ten-dollar room standing empty across the hall, and they wheeled him in on a rolling table pushed by a Negro who said he was Snowball Mason and turned out to be from Warren County too, up around Sixpound, which made Papa feel at home right away and limber enough to flip easy onto the bed in all the clothes he insisted on riding in. But before he could get his breath good, in came a nurse who slid around the bed on her stumpy legs as smooth and speedy as if she was on roller skates with dyed black hair screwed up and bouncing around her ears. She called Papa "darling" as if she had known him all her life and struggled to get him in one of those little night shirts the hospital furnished free without showing everything he had to the whole group. Everybody laughed except Rosacoke who had undressed Papa before and could do it in the dark. She gritted her teeth and finally the nurse got him fixed and stepped back to look as if she had just made him out of thin air. Milo said, "Papa, if you have somebody that peppy around you all the time, you won't be tired long." The nurse smiled and told Papa she would be seeing lots of him in the daytime and then left. Milo laughed at the "lots" and said, "That's what I'm afraid of, Papa—you getting out of hand down here," but Rosacoke said she could manage fine and wasn't exactly a moper herself and Papa agreed to that.

Soon as the nurse got out—after coming back once to get a hairpin she dropped on the bed—they began inspecting the room. There was a good big sink where Rosacoke could rinse out her underwear that she hadn't brought much of and Rato's socks. (Anywhere Rato went he just took the clothes on his back.) And Mama liked the view out the window right over the ambulance entrance where you could see every soul that came in sick. She called Rato's attention to it, and the two of them looked out awhile, but it was getting on towards four o'clock, and much as she wanted to stay and see what Snowball was serving for supper, she told Milo they would have to go. She couldn't stand to ride at night.

Practically before the others left the building, Rosacoke and Rato and Papa had made their sleeping arrangements and were settled. There was one easy chair Rosacoke could sleep in, and since Rato couldn't see stretching out on the floor with his bones, he shoved in another chair out of the parlor down the hall. That dyed-haired nurse saw him do it. She gave him a look that would have dropped anybody but Rato dead in his tracks and said, "You camping out or something, Big Boy?" Rato said, "No'm. Setting with my Papa." Then he went off roaming and the first thing Rosacoke did was open her grip and spread out her toilet articles all over the glass-top bureau. They were all she had brought except for two dresses and a copy of *Hit Parade Tunes and Lyrics* so she could get in some good singing if there was a radio and there was—over Papa's bed, two stations. And at the last minute Mama had stuck in what was left of the saltwater taffy Aunt Oma sent from Virginia Beach that summer. It seemed like a good idea—nurses hung around a patient who had his own candy like Grant around Richmond, Mama said—so she took a piece and gave one to Papa and began to paint her face, trying it out. Papa gummed his candy and watched in the mirror. Mama would have jerked a knot in her if she could have seen the sight Rosacoke was making of herself but Papa smiled. He had always said Rosacoke looked like an actor, and since the only picture show he ever saw was *Birth of a Nation*—and that was forty years ago in the old Warrenton Opera House with a four-piece band in accompaniment—then it must have been Lillian Gish he thought Rosacoke looked like. And she did a little that winter—not as small but thin all the same though beginning to grow, with a heart-shaped face and long yellow hair and blue eyes. That was what Rosacoke liked the best about her face, the eyes. They were big and it was hard to say where the blues left off and the whites began because everything there was more or less blue, and out the far corner of her left eye came this little vein close under the skin that always seemed to Rosacoke to be emptying off some of all that blue, carrying it down to her pale cheek.

But she couldn't stand there staring at herself all the time—she wasn't that good looking and she knew it already—so after the doctors began to ease up with the visits on the second day, Rosacoke got a little tired. That is, till the Volunteer Worker from the Ladies' Guild came in in a pink smock and asked if maybe they wouldn't want some magazines or a deck of cards maybe? She had a pushcart with her full of razor blades and magazines and things, and all Rosacoke had to do was look at Papa, and he—so happy with a lady visitor—pointed to his black leather purse on the table. The best thing she bought was a deck of Bicycle Playing Cards, and Mama would have jerked another knot if she could have seen Rosacoke right in Papa's bed, teaching him to play Honeymoon Bridge and Fish which she had learned awhile back from town girls on rainy days at little recess. But she never mentioned

Slap Jack, her favorite game. She knew in advance Papa would get excited waiting for a Jack to turn up and maybe have a stroke or something so they stuck to quiet games which Papa took to easily, and you could have knocked Rosacoke off the bed with a feather when *he* started teaching her and Rato to play Setback, playing the extra hand himself.

They could count on the cards keeping them busy till Sunday, but they would have to do something with them then. Mama had said she would come down on Sunday to sit her turn with Papa. Milo would bring her after Children's Day. Milo was her oldest boy and he pretty well ran the farm alone with what help Rato could give him. He would probably have to bring Sissie along for the ride even if Papa couldn't stand her. Sissie was Milo's new wife. Just try leaving Sissie anywhere.

THE DOCTORS DIDN'T TELL PAPA WHAT WAS WRONG with him, and he didn't tell them but one thing either which was that he wanted to die at home. He told them they had been mighty nice to him and he appreciated it, but he couldn't think of anything worse than dying away from home. They said they would take care of that and for him to rest till they told him to stop and they would send Dr. Sledge a full report. And Papa didn't worry. He had left it in their hands, and if a doctor had walked in one morning and said he had come to saw his head off, Papa would have just laid his neck out on the pillow where the doctor could get at it. But the doctors didn't bother him for much of his time, and taking them at their word, he slept the best part of every day. That was when Rato would roam the halls, never saying "p-turkey" to anybody, just looking around. And when Rosacoke could see Papa was asleep good, she would tip over and listen to his chest to make sure his heart was beating regular before she would walk across the hall to the corner room, the one they had offered Papa. It was still empty. The door stayed open all the time, and she didn't see any reason for not going in. There was reason *for* going—the view out the window of that room, a white statue of Jesus standing beside the hospital, holding his head bowed down and spreading his hands by his side. His chest was bare and a cloth was hanging over his right shoulder. Rosacoke couldn't see his face too well, but she knew it, clear, from the day they brought Papa in. It was the kindest face she had ever seen. She was sure of that. And she went to that empty room more than once to look out at him and recollect his face the way she knew it was.

But that didn't go on long because on the third day Rato came in from sitting in the hall all morning and said they had just now put some fellow in that empty room. Rosacoke was sorry to hear it. It meant she wouldn't get to go over there in the afternoon any more but she didn't say that. She would rather have died than tell Rato how much time she spent there, looking out a window. Papa wanted to know who it was that could take a twelve-dollar room, and Rato said it was a big man. Papa was disappointed too. He had got it figured there was something wrong with that room, lying empty three days or more. Rato said the man's wife and boy were with him—"I expect it was his boy. Looked like he was anyhow. The man hisself didn't look a bit sick. Walked in on his own steam, talking and laughing." Rosacoke wanted to know if they were rich, but Rato couldn't say, said he didn't know. You couldn't ever tell about Rato though, how much he knew. He wasn't anybody's fool. He just liked the idea of not telling all he knew. Keeping a few secrets was everything Rato had. So Rosacoke said, "Well, he's getting a beautiful room" and then walked over and buttoned Papa's nightshirt. She made him stay buttoned square up to the neck all the time because she couldn't stand to look at his old chest. Papa said he was hot as a mink in Africa and that his chest had been that hairy ever since he shaved it to be Maid of Honor in the womanless wedding Delight Church put on when he was seventeen years old.

THE NIGHT BEFORE, WHEN THE LIGHTS WERE OUT BUT they were still awake, Papa asked Rato to name the best thing he had seen since arriving, and Rato said, "That old lady with all the cards in the big ward down the hall." Rosacoke said, "What sort of cards?" "Every sort there is—Mother's Day, Valentine, Birthday, Christmas..." Papa said, "Get-Well cards?" "She ain't going to get well. She's too old." Rosacoke said "How old?" and Rato said, "What's the oldest thing you know?" She thought and said "God." "Well, she's something similar to that." Rosacoke and Papa laughed but Rato said, "I'm telling the truth. Go take a look if you get the chance. She sleeps all the time." Then they went to sleep but Rosacoke knew he was telling the truth, and anyhow he spoke of his doings so seldom she thought she would take his advice. So the afternoon the man took the twelve-dollar room, she went down while Papa was nodding, and at first it looked the way Rato promised. There was a lady older than God in the bed by the door (saving her a walk past nine other beds), covered to the chin and flat as a plank with no pillow under her head, just steel-colored hair laid wild on the sheets. Rosacoke stepped close enough to see her eyes were shut, and thinking the lady was asleep, she looked up towards a sunburst of greeting cards fanned on the wall over the bed, but she hadn't looked fifteen seconds when the lady shot bolt-upright and spoke in a voice like a fingernail scraping down a dry blackboard—"Praise my Jesus." Rosacoke said "Yes'm" and the lady smiled and said, "Step here, honey, and take a seat and I'll tell you how I got saved at age eighty-one in the midst of a meeting of two hundred people. Then I'll show you my cards—sent by my Sunday school class and my many friends"—and commenced scratching her hair. But Rosacoke said, "No thank you, ma'm" and walked out quicker than she came. She went a few feet outside the door and stopped and thought, "I ought to be ashamed, getting her hopes up. I ought to go back and let her talk." Then she heard the lady's voice scraping on to the empty air so she said to herself, "If I went for five minutes, I'd be there all afternoon, hearing about her cards. Papa is *my* duty." And anyhow she didn't like the lady. It was fine for your friends to send you cards, but that was no reason to organize a show as if you were the only person in the hospital with that many friends and all of them with nothing in the world to do but sit down and write you cards all day. She thought that out and then headed for Papa.

She was walking down the mile-long hall when she saw him—not right at first. At first she was too busy looking at people laid back with their doors open. She didn't know a one of them, not even their faces the way Rato did. The only thing she knew was Snowball Mason in one room, talking to some old man that looked so small in his little outing pajamas with his legs hanging off the bed no more than an inch from the floor like thin dry tan gourds swinging in a wind on somebody's back porch somewhere. Snowball saw her and remembered her as being from Warren County and bowed. She stopped to talk but she happened to look towards the left, and there he was—Wesley—sitting way down across from Papa's door, dressed to the ears and watching the floor the way he always did, not studying people. Still he had come sixty miles to see her so she whispered to Snowball she had to go and went to meet Wesley, holding back from running and trying not to look as if she had seen a ghost which was close to what she had seen, considering this was the last hope she had. He hadn't seen her yet and she could surprise him. She hadn't really missed him so much till now, but when she got nearer she knew how sorry she would be to miss this Saturday with him, and she speeded her steps but kept them quiet. She was almost on him and he put his hands across his eyes—it would be Wesley all over to go to sleep waiting for her—so she came up to him and smiled and said, "Good afternoon, Mr. Beavers, is there something I can do for you?"

But it wasn't Wesley at all. It was somebody she

hadn't ever seen before, somebody who didn't really look very much like Wesley when she thought about it. It took whoever it was a little while to realize she was speaking to him, and when he looked up he looked sad and nearly as young as Rosacoke. He looked a little blank too, the way everybody does when you have called them by the wrong name and they don't want you to know it. In a minute he said, "Oh no ma'm, thank you." "No ma'm"—as if Rosacoke was some kind of nurse.

It just about killed her to have done that like some big hussy. The only thing left to say was "Excuse me," and she almost didn't get that out before shutting Papa's door behind her, the hot blood knocking in her ears. Papa was still asleep but Rato was standing by the window, having some Nabs and a Pepsi for dinner, and when she could speak she said would he please peep out and see who that was sitting in the hall. As if Rato had ever peeped in his life. He had done plenty of looking but no peeping so he just pulled open the door as if he was headed for dinner and gave the boy a look. Before he got the door closed good, he said, "Nobody but that man's boy from across the hall. That man they moved in today." Rosacoke said "Thank you" and later on that afternoon she wondered if since he looked like Wesley, that boy could say goodbye like Wesley could.

IF THEY DIDN'T DO ANYTHING ELSE, THOSE PEOPLE across the hall at least gave Papa something to think about. They kept their door shut all the time except when somebody was going or coming, and even then they were usually too quick for Rato to get a good enough look to report anything. Something was bound to be wrong though because of all the nurses and doctors hanging around and the way that boy looked whenever he walked out in the hall for a few minutes. Rato reported he saw the man's wife once. He said she was real pretty and looked like she was toting the burden of the world on her shoulders. Even Rato could tell that. So Papa couldn't help asking Snowball the next time he got a chance what was wrong with that man. Snowball said he didn't know and if he did he wouldn't be allowed to say and that made Papa mad. He knew Snowball spent about two-thirds of his time in the man's room, taking bedpans in and out, and he told Snowball at the top of his voice, "That white coat you got on has gone to your head." Rosacoke could have crawled under the bed, but there was no stopping Papa once he got started. You just pretended hadn't a thing happened and he would quiet down. She could tell it got Snowball's goat though and she was sorry. He walked out of Papa's room with his ice-cream coat hanging off him as if somebody had unstarched it.

But that evening when it was time for him to go home, Snowball came back in. He didn't have his white coat on, and that meant he was off duty. He had on his sheepish grin, trying to show he had come on a little social call to see how Papa was making out, but Rosacoke knew right off he had come to apologize to Papa who was taking a nap so she shook Papa and said Snowball wanted to speak to him. Papa raised up blinking and said "Good evening, Snow," and Rosacoke couldn't help smiling at how Snowball turned into a snake doctor, dipping up and down around Papa. He said he just wondered how Mr. Mustian was coming on this afternoon, and did they have any old newspapers he could take home to start fires with? Papa said he was tolerable and hadn't looked at a newspaper since the jimpson weeds took over the Government. What he meant was the Republicans, and he said, "The bad thing about jimpson weeds, Snow, is they reseeds theyselves."

Snowball hadn't come in on his own time to hear that though, and it didn't take him long to work his way to Papa's bed and lean over a lot closer than Papa liked for anybody to get to him and say it the same way he would have told a secret. "Mr. Mustian, they fixing to take out that gentleman's lung."

"What you talking about?"

"That Mr. Ledwell yonder in the room across the hall. He got a eating-cancer. That's what I hear his nurse say. But don't tell nobody. I just thought you might want to know so soons I found out . . ."

"A eating-cancer? That's what it is?"

"They don't seem to be no doubt about it. I done already shaved his chest for surgery. He taking his operation in the morning at eight."

Papa wanted to know, "Is he going to live, Snowball?"

"Can't say, Mr. Mustian. He spit the first blood today, and alls I know is they ain't many lives past that. They ain't many. And if they lives you almost wish they hadn't. That's how bad they gets before it's over."

And Papa remembered that was the way it was with Mr. Jack Rooker who swelled up to twice his natural size and smelled a long time before he died. "I can recollect sitting on the porch in the evening and hearing Jack Rooker screaming clean across two tobacco fields, screaming for his oldest boys to just let him rest because there wasn't nothing nobody could do for him, not nothing. And I'd say to Pauline, 'Pauline, it don't look like Jack Rooker is ever going to die, does it?'" But that was a long time ago when Papa was a lot younger and a lot farther away from dying himself. That was why he could feel so for Jack Rooker back then. It had just seemed as if Jack Rooker was going through something wouldn't anybody else ever have to go through again.

Snowball was nodding his head up and down, saying, "I know. Yes sir, I know," but Rosacoke could tell he had made his peace with Papa and was ready to leave so she stopped Papa from running on about Jack Rooker and told him it was time for Snowball to go home. Papa thanked Snowball for coming in, as if he had never been mad a minute, and said he would count on him keeping them posted on all that happened to that fellow across the hall.

Rosacoke followed Snowball out. "Snowball, what's that man's name again?"

"Mr. Ledwell."

"Is he really going to die, you think?"

"Yes'm, I believe he is. But Miss Rosacoke, you don't have to worry yourself none about that. You ain't going to see him."

"I know that. I just wondered though. I didn't even remember his name."

Snowball said he would be stepping along and would see her in the morning. But Rosacoke didn't hear from him till way in the next afternoon. Papa was taking his nap and she was almost asleep herself when

Snowball peeped in and seeing Papa was asleep, whispered that the gentleman across the hall was back from his operation.

"How did it come out, Snow?"

"They tell me he is doing right well, Miss Rosacoke."

"Has he waked up yet?"

"No'm, he lying in yonder under his oxygen tent, running on about all sorts of foolishness like a baby. He be in some pain when he do come to though."

"Are his people doing all right?"

"They holding up right well. That's his two sisters with his wife and his boy. They setting there looking at him and waiting to see."

She thanked Snowball for letting them know and said she would tell Papa when he woke up. After Snowball left she stepped into the hall herself. The door over there was closed, and for the first time it said "No visitors." She wanted to wait until somebody opened it. Then she could at least hear the man breathing, if he was still breathing. But there wasn't a sound coming through the oak door thick as her fist, and she wasn't going to be caught snooping like Rato so she went back in to where Papa was awake, spreading a game of Solitaire which that dyed-haired nurse had taught him to play. That was *all* she had done for him.

SINCE THEY WERE AWAY FROM HOME, THEY WENT TO bed around ten o'clock. That is they cut out the lights, and Rosacoke would step in the closet and undress with the door half shut. The first evening she had shut it all the way, and Papa told her there was no use to be so worried about him seeing her as he had seen her stripstrod naked two or three hundred times before she was old enough to walk, but she kept up the practice, and when she was in her nightgown, she would step out and kiss Papa and tell Rato "Sleep tight" and settle in her easy chair under a blanket. Then they would talk a little about the day and home till the talk ran down of its own accord though Papa was liable to go on another hour in the dark about things he remembered. But it would be all quiet soon enough, and Rato would be the first to sleep. After Rosacoke's eyes had opened full to the dark, she could look over and see her brother stretched sideways in his chair, still dressed, with his long hands caught between his drawn-up knees and his head rolled back on his great thin neck and his mouth fallen open. Most people seemed to be somebody else when they were asleep. But not Rato. Rato went to sleep the way you expected he would, like himself who had stopped looking for a while. Then Papa would fall off, sometimes right in the middle of what he was remembering, and Rosacoke could see him too, but he was different—sweeter and with white hair that seemed in the night to be growing into the white pillow his dark leather head rested on, holding him there forever.

After Papa slept Rosacoke was supposed to but she couldn't this night. She kept thinking about it, the man and his boy. Papa had forgotten all about Mr. Ledwell. She hadn't told him anything about the operation, and she had asked Snowball not to tell him, either. She didn't want Papa to start back thinking and talking about that poor man and asking questions and sending Rato out to see what he could. She had it all to

herself now. Snowball had told her Mr. Ledwell's boy
was staying there with him through the nights. Mr.
Ledwell had made the boy promise him that before he
would go to the operating room, and the boy would be
over there now, awake maybe with his father that was
dying and she here on her chair trying to sleep with her
Papa and Rato, her Papa turned into something else in
the night.

Still she might have gone on to sleep if she hadn't
thought of Wesley. If she was at home she could go to
sleep knowing she would see Wesley at seven-thirty in
the morning. He drove the schoolbus and went nearly
four miles out of his way on the state's gas to pick her
up first so they could talk alone a few minutes before
they looked up and saw all those Gupton children in
the road, knocking together in the cold and piling on
the bus not saying a word with purple splotches like
thick cobwebs down their legs that came from standing
by an open fire, Mama said, and in winter afternoons
Wesley would put her out last into the cold white yard
that would be nearly dark by five, and she would walk
on towards the light that was coming already from the
kitchen windows, steamed on the inside like panes of
ice stretched thin on frames. And huddled there she
thought how Wesley had said they would go to Warrenton this coming Saturday for a traveling show spon-
sored by the Lions Club—an exact copy of the Florida
State Electric Chair with some poor dummy strapped
in it, waiting for the end. Wesley was interested in anything mechanical, and she would have gone with him
(no charge for admission the paper said, just a chance
to help the Club's Blind Fund) if that was how he
wanted to pass time—striking up friends with the

owner of the chair whoever it was and talking till time to head back home. But that would have been all right with Rosacoke. She would have waited and been glad if she had got the chance, but she wouldn't now and like as not Wesley would take Willie Duke Aycock which was what Willie Duke had waited for all her life. That was just Wesley. Let her miss school even two days at hog killing and he practically forgot her.

It was thinking all this that kept Rosacoke from going on to sleep. She tried once or twice to empty her head the way she could sometimes at home by closing her eyes and thinking way out in front of her, but she couldn't manage that tonight so she listened till she heard slow breathing from Rato and Papa. Then she got up in her bare feet and felt for the closet door and took down her robe from a hook and put it on. It was peach-colored chenille. She had made it herself and it had been honorable mention at the 4-H Fall Dress Revue in the Warren County Armory. She took her shoes in her hand and opened the door. The hall was empty and the only light was the one at the nurses' desk, and that was so white, shining into both ends of the long hall and against the white charts hanging in tiers. The two night nurses were gone or she could have talked to them. She hadn't ever talked to them, but they seemed nice enough not to mind if she did want to talk. She guessed they were out giving sleeping pills so she walked towards the big ward to pass time.

It was dark down there and all these sounds came out to meet her a long time before she got to the door like some kind of Hell she was hearing from a long way away—a little moan strained out through old dry lips and the grating of each private snore as it tore its way up the throats of the ones who were already asleep. Rosacoke stopped in the open door. The nurses were not there. Nobody seemed to be walking in the dark anyhow. All she could really see was, close to the door, an old woman set up in bed, bent all over on herself and scratching at her hair real slow. But she knew the others were there, and she knew there ought to be something you could do for such people, something you could say even in the dark that would make them know why you were standing there looking—not because you were well yourself and just trying to walk yourself to sleep but because you felt for them, because you hadn't ever been that sick or that old or that alone before in all your life and because you wished they hadn't been either. You couldn't stand there and say to the whole room out loud, "Could I bring you all some ice water or something?" because they probably wouldn't want that anyhow, and even if they did the first ones would be thirsty again and pitching in their hot sheets before you could make it around the room. You would be there all night, and it would be like trying to fill up No-Bottom Pond if it was ever to get empty. So she turned in the open door and saw one nurse back at the desk and walked in that direction, stopping to look at the flowers waiting outside the room of an old man who said they breathed up too much good air at night.

She was some way off when she saw the man's boy. There was no doubt about it being him this time and she was not surprised. The boy walked fast towards the desk, his shirt open down the front, the white tails sweeping behind him in the light of the one lamp and his chest deep brown almost as if he had worked in the field but you knew he hadn't. When he got to the nurse he shut his eyes and said, "My father's nurse says please call Dr. Davis and tell him to come now. It's serious." His voice was low and fast but Rosacoke heard him. The nurse took her time staring at a list of numbers under the glass on her desk before she called. She told whoever she talked to that Mr. Ledwell had taken a turn for the worse. Then she stood and walked to his room. The boy went close behind her so she stopped at the door and said "Wait out here." When she shut the door it stirred enough breeze to lift his shirttail again. He was that close and without stepping back he stood awhile looking. Then he sat by the door where Rosacoke had seen him the first awful time.

She looked on at it from the dark end of the hall (she was not walking by him in her robe even if it had won honorable mention), but she saw him plain because a table was by his chair and he had switched on a small study lamp that lighted his tired face. His chin hung on his hand like dead weight on delicate scales and his eyes were shut. Rosacoke knew if he looked towards the dark he might see her—at least her face —and she pressed to the blackest wall and watched from there. For a long time he was still. No noise came through his father's door. Then clear as day a woman's voice spoke in the open ward, "I have asked and asked for salt on my dinner"—spoke it twice, not changing a word. Some other voice said "Hush" and the boy faced right and looked. Rosacoke didn't know if he saw her or not (maybe he was just seeing dark) but she saw him—his eyes, far off as she was, and they were the saddest eyes in the world to Rosacoke, that pulled hard at her and called on her or just on the dark to do

something soon. But she didn't. She couldn't after the
mistake of that first time. She shuddered in the hard
waves that flushed over her whole body and locked her
there in the shadow. Once she put out her hand and
her foot and took one small step towards the boy
whose head had dropped onto his folded arms, but the
bleached light struck her robe, and she dropped back
the way one of those rain snails does that is feeling its
path, damp and tender, across the long grass till you
touch its gentle horns, and it draws itself back, hurt
and afraid, into a tight piece you would never guess
could think or move or feel, even.

She couldn't have said how long she stood there,
getting so tired she knew how it felt to be dead, before
the doctor they called came in. He didn't have a tie on,
and sleep was in his eyes. He saw the boy and touched
him and said something, and they both walked into the
room. Before they shut the door a sound like a mad
child catching at his breath after crying ran out behind
them to where Rosacoke was. She didn't know what
was happening, but the boy's father might be dying.
She knew that much. She felt almost sure that if the
man died they would make some kind of public an-
nouncement. But he didn't die and she had waited so
long she was nearly asleep. The hall she had to walk
through back to Papa's was as quiet now as a winter
night in an attic room when you could look out the
window and see a sky, cold and hard as a worn plow
point shining with the moon. All those people in the
ward were asleep or maybe they had given up trying
and waited. It seemed as if when you waited at night
for something—maybe you didn't know what—the

only thing happened was, time made noise in a clock somewhere way off.

IT WAS THE NEXT MORNING THAT ROSACOKE MADE up her mind. If Mr. Ledwell had lived through the night, she was going to call on him and his family. It was the only thing to do, the only Christian thing to do—to go over there and introduce yourself and ask if there was anything you could do to help such as setting up at night. The way she felt she might have gone over that morning if the room hadn't been so quiet. She hadn't seen a soul come or go since she woke up. She didn't know how Mr. Ledwell was getting along after everything that happened the night before. She didn't know if he had lived out the night. All she could do was wait for Snowball to tell her. She wasn't going to ask Rato to do any more looking for her after the last time.

Snowball was late coming by that morning, but he got there finally and called her out in the hall to talk. He said Mr. Ledwell had a relapse the night before, and they thought he was passing away, but he pulled through unexpectedly. "He not going to last though, Miss Rosacoke. The day nurse tell me he full of cancer. It's a matter of days, they say, and he know that hisself so all of us try to keep his spirits up. He ain't a old man. I old enough to be his Daddy. He resting right easy this morning, but he was bad sick last night. In fact he was dead for a few minutes before the doctor come and brought him around. They does that right often now you know."

That made Rosacoke think of the day the Phelps boy fell off the dam at Fleming's Mill backwards into twenty feet of water, and three men who were fishing dived in in all their clothes and found his body face-down on the bottom and dragged it out, the mouth hanging open in one corner as if a finger was pulling it down. He had stayed under water four or five minutes, and his chest and wrists were still. They said he was dead as a hammer for half an hour till one man pumped air in him and he belched black mud and began to moan through his teeth. But what Rosacoke always wondered was, where did they go if they died for a while—Mr. Ledwell and the drowned Phelps boy —and if you were to ask them, could they tell you where they had been and what it was like there or had they just been to sleep? She had heard that somebody asked the Phelps boy when he got well enough to go back to school what dying was like, and he said he couldn't tell because it was a secret between him and his Jesus. Mama had said that was all you could expect out of a Phelps anyhow—that she wouldn't ask him if you paid her cash money and that you couldn't just suppose he had gone to Heaven and if he hadn't, you could be sure he wouldn't admit going elsewhere. (She had smiled but she meant it. She had never had a kind word for that branch of Phelpses since they bootlegged their way to big money some years before.) But not everybody felt the way Mama did. A church of Foot-Washing Baptists up towards South Hill heard about it and invited the boy up to testify but he wouldn't go. And from then on Rosacoke had watched him as if he was something not quite natural that had maybe seen Hell with his own eyes and had lived to tell the tale— or not tell it—and she had followed after him at little recess, hiding where he couldn't notice her so she could watch his face close up and see if his wonderful experience had made him any different. As it turned out it had. He was the quietest thing you could imagine, and his eyes danced all the time as if he was remembering and you couldn't ever know what, not ever.

By the time Rosacoke thought that, Snowball had to leave, but before he went she asked what he thought about her going over to see Mr. Ledwell and his family.

"It couldn't do no harm I can think of, Miss Rosacoke, if you don't stay but a little while. He can't talk much with his one lung, but he be happy to have a visitor. You wait though till he get a little of his strength back from last night."

She nodded Yes but she hadn't planned to pay her visit that morning anyhow. She had made up her mind not to go over there till she could take something with her. She might be from Afton, N.C., but she knew better than to go butting into some man's sickroom, to a man on his deathbed, without an expression of her sympathy. And it had to be flowers. There was that much she could do for Mr. Ledwell because he didn't have friends. He and his family had moved to Raleigh less than six months ago. Snowball had found out the Ledwells were from Baltimore. But of course there wasn't a flower for sale anywhere in the hospital, and anyhow it wasn't cut flowers Rosacoke had in mind. She got a dime from Papa by saying it was time she sent Mama word as to how they were getting along. Then she hunted down one of the Volunteers and bought two cards with the Capitol on them. She wrote one to Mama.

Dear Mama,
    We like it here alot. I hope you and Baby Sister, Milo and Sissie are all O.K. Papa and I are getting plenty rest. Rato is the one taking exercise. When you come down here would you bring some of your altheas if they have bloomed yet?

                                    Yours truly,
                                    Rosacoke Mustian

She wrote the other one to Wesley Beavers.

Dear Wesley,
    How are you getting along? I am fine but miss you alot. Do you miss me? When you go to see the Florida Electric Chair think of how much I would like to be there. If you see Willie Duke Aycock tell her I said hello. I hope to see you Monday early.

                                    Your friend,
                                    Rosacoke

Then she mailed them and waited and hoped the altheas had bloomed. Mama had got an idea out of *Life* magazine that you could force things to flower in winter, and she had dug up an althea bush and set it in a tub and put it in the kitchen by the stove and dared it not to bloom. If it had she would gladly pick a handful of oily purple flowers that bruised if you touched them and hold them in her big lap the whole way to Raleigh on Sunday.

AND SUNDAY CAME BEFORE ROSACOKE WAS READY. She woke up early enough (Rato saw to that—he could wake the dead just tying his shoes), but she took her time getting washed and dressed, straightening the

room and hiding things away. She didn't expect the
family till after dinner so it was nearly noon before she
set Papa up and lathered his face and started to shave
him. She had finished one side without a nick, singing
as she worked—the radio was on to the final hymn at
Tabernacle Baptist Church—when the door burst
open, and there was Baby Sister and Mama close behind her with flowers. Baby Sister said "Here I am."
Rosacoke got her breath and said, "Blow me down.
We sure didn't look for you early as this. Mama, I
thought you had Children's Day to get behind you before you could leave."

Mama kissed her and touched Papa's wrist. "I did. I
did. But once I pulled the Sunbeams through 'Come
and Sing Some Happy Happy Song,' I felt like I could
leave so we didn't stay to hear Bracey Overby end it
with Taps. I know he did all right though. I hope he
did—he practiced till he was pale anyhow. Then after
leaving church like Indians in the middle of everything
to get here early of course some Negroes drove up at
the house just as we was starting—some of those cur-
ious Marmaduke Negroes with red hair. Well, they had
heard about Baby Sister, and they had this skinny baby
and wanted her to blow down his throat." (Negroes
were always doing that. A child who had never seen
its father could cure sore throat by breathing on it.)
"It's a awful thing but Baby Sister enjoys it—don't
you?—and I can't deny her any powers she may have
especially on Sunday." (Nobody had denied Baby
Sister—six years old and big for the name—anything
she wanted since she was born six months to the day
after her father died. Even the nurses didn't try. Mama
marched her in past a dozen signs that plainly said *No*

Children Under 12 and Baby Sister in Sweetheart Pink
and nobody uttered a sound.) All through her story
Mama looked around, and when she was done she said
"Where is Rato?"

Rosacoke said, "Patrolling, I guess. He'll show up
for dinner," and before she could wonder where were
Milo and Sissie, they strolled in from parking the car.
Milo kissed Rosacoke and said, "Wesley sent you
that." Mama said, "No he didn't. We haven't seen
Wesley." Then he laughed and kissed Papa—"Miss
Betty Upchurch sent you that, but I don't tickle as
good as her." (Miss Betty was a crazy old widow with
whiskers that he teased Papa about.) Everybody
laughed except Sissie. When they quieted down Sissie
said "Good morning" and showed her teeth and settled back to looking as if a Mack truck had hit her
head-on so Milo explained it to Papa. "Sissie will be
off the air today. She's mad—woke up mad but didn't
find reasons till we were leaving home. Then she found
two good ones. One was she had to shell butter beans
all the way up here because Mama didn't read the di-
rections and froze her damn beans in the shell. The
other thing was that she had to sit on the backseat to
do it because Mama and Baby Sister had spoke to sit
up front with me and the heater. Well, she sat back
there shelling, and when she finished—it took her a
hour and we were on the outskirts of Raleigh—she
lowered the glass on her side, intending to empty out
the hulls, but Baby Sister said, 'Shut that pneumonia
hole,' and Sissie got flustered and threw out the beans
instead. Mama capped the climax by laughing, and
Sissie ain't spoke a word since except just now." He
turned to Sissie who was already staring out the win-

dow—"Say something, Doll Baby. Turn over a new leaf." She wouldn't even look so Milo laughed and that did seal her. It was a good thing. Nobody could make Papa madder than Sissie when she started running her mouth.

Mama frowned at Milo and said, "Everybody calm down. We got half a day to get through in this matchbox." She meant Papa's room that was ten by twelve. Then she went to the bureau and while Rosacoke scraped chairs around, she took off her hat and her white ear bobs and combed her hair and put on a hairnet and slipped off her shoes. She went to the chair where Rato slept—in her stocking feet—and said, "Rosacoke, get me my bed shoes out of my grip." Rosacoke got them. Then Mama settled back and blew one time with relief. She had come to stay and she had brought three things with her—dinner for seven in a cardboard suit box, her grip, and enough altheas to fill a zinc tub. She made it plain right away that Rosacoke would go on home with Milo and Sissie and Baby Sister but Rato would stay on to help her with Papa. Milo said he planned on leaving between eight and nine o'clock. (What he had in mind was to pacify Sissie by taking her to supper at the Chinese café she liked so much and then going on to a Sunday picture. But he didn't tell Mama that.) And Rosacoke couldn't object to leaving. In some ways she would be glad to get home, and Milo's plans would give her time to pay her visit to Mr. Ledwell, time to do all she wanted to do, all she thought she could do—to step over when she had seen her family and pay her respects and give them the flowers that would say better than she could how much she felt for Mr. Ledwell, dying in this

strange place away from his friends and his home, and
for his people who were waiting.

So she had that day with her family (Rato appeared
long enough for dinner), and the day went fine except
for three things. One thing was Sissie but nobody ever
looked for Sissie to act decent. Another thing was,
after they had eaten the dinner Mama packed, Papa
reached over to his bedside table and pulled out the
playing cards. Rosacoke had taken pains to hide them
way back in the drawer, but Papa pulled them out in
full view and set up a game of Solitaire and looked at
Mama and grinned. She made a short remark about it
appeared to her Papa was learning fancy tricks in his
old age. Papa said couldn't he teach her a few games,
and she drew up in her chair and said she had gone
nearly fifty years—seven of them as a deaconess in
Delight Baptist Church—without knowing one playing
card from the other, and she guessed she could live on
in ignorance the rest of the time. But she didn't stop
Papa. He just stopped offering to teach her and lay
there the rest of the afternoon, dealing out hands of
Solitaire till he was blue in the face. He played right on
through the nap everybody took after dinner. You
couldn't have stopped him with dynamite. The third
thing was after their naps. When they all woke up it
was nearly three-thirty and the natural light was dim.
Rosacoke stood up to switch on the bulb, but Milo said
"No don't," and even closed the blinds. Then he went
to Papa and pointed at his necktie and said, "Watch
this. Pretty soon it'll start lighting up." It was something he had got that week by mail, and he claimed it
would say "Kiss Me In The Dark!" when the room got
dim enough, but they waited and the only thing the tie

did was shine pale green all over. Rosacoke was glad he didn't get it working but Papa was disappointed. He asked Milo to leave the tie with him so he could test it in total darkness and show it around to the nurses, but Milo said he was intending to wear it to some crop-dusting movies at the high school that coming Thursday.

In a few more minutes it was five o'clock, and Milo started his plans by saying he and Sissie were going for a little ride and for Rosacoke to be packed for home by nine. Then he got Sissie up and into her coat and they left. Whenever Milo left a place things always quieted down. Papa went back to his Solitaire, and Mama crocheted on a tablecloth that she said would be Rosacoke's wedding present if the thread didn't rot beforehand. Even Baby Sister, who had pestered all afternoon to make up for Sissie being on strike, was worn out and sat still, sucking her thumb, so in the quiet room Rosacoke took down her grip and packed in almost everything. But she kept out her only clean dress and took it down to the nurses' utility closet and pressed it and put it on. She had washed it in the hall bathtub the night before. When she came back to the room, nobody paid her any mind. They thought she was just getting ready to go home. She washed her hands and face and stood in front of the mirror, combing her hair and working up her nerve. She turned her back to Mama and put on a little lipstick and rouge to keep from looking so pale. Then she took the altheas up out of the water Mama set them in and dried the stems with a clean towel and wrapped tissue paper around them. Mama said, "You are dressing too soon," and Rosacoke said, "I reckon I am," but before anybody had seen her good, she slipped out the door in her yellow dress, holding the flowers. She had tied a white card to them. Snowball had got it for her the day before. It said "From a Friend Across the Hall."

SHE TOOK THREE STEPS AND STOPPED AND STOOD IN front of the oak door, taller than she would ever be, that said "Ledwell." Behind it was where Mr. Ledwell was and his people that she didn't know, where he had laid down that first day Rato saw him talking and laughing, where he had gone out from to take his operation, and where it was not his home. Rosacoke was nervous but she told herself she looked as good as she could, and she had the altheas in her hands to hide the shaking. She knocked on the door and she must have knocked too soft because nobody came. She knocked again and put her ear to the wood. There were dim sounds coming from the other side so she pushed the door open a little, but the room was dark and quiet as an open field at night with only the sky, and she was drawing back to leave when the moving light of candles caught her, streaming from a part of the room she couldn't see into, drawing her on. So she went inside and pressed the door silent behind her and stood up against it, waiting till her eyes had opened enough to halfway see. There were five or six people in the room. Mr. Ledwell was a ridge on the bed that the sheets rose and fell over in gullies like after a rain, and his boy was by his head, holding one of the candles. In the yellow light the boy looked a way Wesley Beavers might never look, and the same light fell through a clear tent that covered his father's head and chest. A little of it fell on three ladies off in a corner,

kneeling on the hard floor, and on a man standing near
the bed by a table with two candles on it. He was all in
black and falling from his neck was a narrow band of
purple cloth with fine gold crosses at the ends. He was
talking in words Rosacoke didn't know, almost singing
in a voice that was low and far away because he was
old with white hair and was looking down, but finally
he looked up at Mr. Ledwell's boy, and the two of
them pulled the tent back off him. Rosacoke knew he
was alive. She could hear the air sucking into his
throat, and his eyes were open on the boy and on the
yellow candle.

The old man in black moved his hands in the air
three times carefully, wide and long over Mr. Ledwell.
Then he took a piece of cotton and waited for Mr.
Ledwell to shut his eyes. He wiped the cotton over the
lids, and they were shining for a second, wet and slick
under the light before Mr. Ledwell opened them again
and turned them back to the boy. The boy rolled his
father's head to one side and then to the other while
the old man touched the cotton to the ears that looked
cold, and all the time Mr. Ledwell was trying not to
take his eyes off the boy as if that sad face in the soft
light that came and went was what kept him from
dying. And except for that same soft light, the walls of
the room would have disappeared and the ceiling, and
Rosacoke could have walked out through where the
window had been that she used to stand by. It seemed
to be time for her to leave anyhow. She didn't know
how long this would go on. She didn't know what it
was. She only knew they were getting Mr. Ledwell
ready to die in their own way, and she had taken the
first step to leave when the boy's face turned and saw

her through all that dark. His face changed for a minute, and you might have thought he smiled if you hadn't known that couldn't have happened now, not on his face. That was why Rosacoke didn't leave. He had looked at her as if he knew why she was there, almost as if he would have needed her if there had been time. But the old man touched Mr. Ledwell's lips, and Mr. Ledwell strained his head off the pillow and sucked at the cotton before the old man could pull it back. He thought they were giving him something to drink. And it went on that way over his hands that had to be pulled out from under the cover and his feet that seemed to be tallow you could gouge a line in with your fingernail. When they finished with his head, they put the tent back over him, and Rosacoke couldn't hear his breathing quite so loud. From his feet the old man walked back to his head. He put a black wood cross that had Jesus, white and small, nailed on it into Mr. Ledwell's hand. Then he shook a fine mist of water over him and made the sign again, and Rosacoke heard words she could understand. The old man told Mr. Ledwell to say, "Thy will be done." Mr. Ledwell nodded his head and his eyes opened. He took his hand and tapped on the inside of the clear tent. When his boy looked at him, his voice came up in pieces— but Rosacoke heard him plain—"Don't forget to give Jack Rowan one of those puppies." The boy said he wouldn't forget. Mr. Ledwell looked easier and when the old man reached under the tent to take the cross and Jesus away from him, he nodded his head over and over as he turned the cross loose.

The old man went over to speak to the lady who must have been Mr. Ledwell's wife. She was still on

her knees, and she never took her face out of her
hands. That was when Rosacoke left. They might
switch on the light, and there she would be looking on
at this dying which was the most private thing in the
world. She had stayed that long because the boy had
looked at her, but he might have forgotten by now. He
had never looked again. A chair was by the door. She
laid her flowers there. In the light somebody might see
them and be glad that whoever it was stepped over to
bring them, stepped over without saying a word.

SHE WAITED IN THE HALL FOR THE SOUND OF HIS
dying because he had seemed so ready, but it didn't
come—nobody came or went but a colored girl, pushing a cartload of supper towards the ward—so she had
to walk back into Papa's room, dreading questions.
The room was dim though and still with only the light
over Papa's bed that shined on his hair and the cards
spread out on his knees. But he was just turning them
over now, not really playing, and when Rosacoke shut
the door, he looked and put one finger to his mouth
and pointed towards Baby Sister, asleep at last in
Mama's lap, and Mama nodding. Rosacoke thought
she was safe and halfway smiled and leaned on the
door, waiting for breath. But Papa stared at her and
then tried to whisper—"You are leaving me, ain't
you?"—and Mama jerked awake. It took her a while
to get her bearings, but finally she said, "Where in the
world have you been with Papa's flowers?" Rosacoke
said, "To see a friend." Papa said, "I didn't want no
flowers. Who is your friend?" She said "Mr. Ledwell"
but Papa didn't show recollection. Mr. Ledwell hadn't
crossed his mind since the operation, but just to say

something he asked was the man coming on all right?
Rosacoke said, "He ain't doing so good, Papa" and to
Mama who had never had a secret, never wanted one,
"Mama, please don't ask me who that is because I
don't know."

Then she went to her grip and turned her back on
the room and began packing in the things she had left
till last. She was almost done when Rato walked in.
Nobody had seen Rato since dinner. He walked in and
said it the way he might walk in the kitchen and drop a
load of wood in the box—"That man over yonder is
dead. Ain't been five minutes." Mama said she was
always sorry to hear of any death, and Rato said if
they left the door cracked open they could see the man
because a nurse had already called the undertaker to
come after the body. But Rosacoke faced him and said
"No" and said it so Rato wouldn't dare to crack the
door one inch. He just left fast and slammed it behind
him. But Baby Sister slept through it all, and Mama
didn't speak for fear of disturbing her so the room was
still again. To keep her hands busy Rosacoke rear-
ranged the few little things in her grip, but she stood
sideways to look at Papa and have him to fill her mind.
Papa had his cards that he went back to, but he dealt
them slow because he was thinking. He was so old
himself you couldn't expect him to be too sad. Lately
he always said he knew so many more dead men than
live ones that there wasn't a soul left who could call
him by his first name. And that was the truth. That
was what took the edge off death for Papa—grieving
over so many people, so many of his friends, burying
so much love with each one of them till he had buried
them all (everybody he had nearly) and pretty nearly

all his love, and death didn't hold fear for him anymore. It wasn't as if he didn't know where he was
going or what it would be like when he got there. He
just trusted and he hoped for one thing, he tried to see
to one last thing—for a minute he stopped his card
playing and asked Mama could he die at home, and
Mama told him he could.

That was what made Rosacoke think so long about
Mr. Ledwell who had died in that dark room. She
wouldn't be able to go to his funeral, wouldn't even be
asked. But that wasn't so bad. She had done what she
could, being away from home, hadn't she, and didn't
she know his name at least and hadn't he died not cut
up or shot or run over but almost in his sleep with his
wife and his boy there, and with all that beautiful
dying song, hadn't he surely died sanctified? If he had
to die wasn't that as good a way as any, leaving his
living picture back here in that boy? But she hadn't
ever seen him alive really. She hadn't ever told him or
any of his kind—out loud—that she felt for them. She
hadn't ever said it so loud she could hear her own
voice—that Rosacoke Mustian was sorry to see it hap-
pen. That was why she spoke at last. She had been
quiet so long, and now her slow lean voice cut through
all the dark in the room. "It don't seem right," she
said. "It just don't seem right. It seem like I had got to
know him real well." And her words hung in the room
for a long time—longer than it took Papa to pick the
cards up off the bed and lay them without a sound in
the drawer, longer even than it would have taken Rosacoke to say goodbye to Wesley if it had been Saturday night and she had been at home.

THE WARRIOR
PRINCESS OZIMBA

S HE WAS THE OLDEST THING ANY OF US KNEW
anything about, and she had never been near a
tennis court, but somewhere around the Fourth
of July every year, one of us (it was my father for a
long time but for the past two years, just me) rode out
to her place and took her a pair of blue tennis shoes.
(Blue because that was her favorite color before she
went blind and because even now, opening the box and
not seeing them, she always asked "Is they blue?") We
did it on the Fourth because that was the day she had
picked out fifty years ago for her birthday, not knowing what day she had been born and figuring that the
Fourth was right noisy anyhow and one more little cel-
ebration wouldn't hurt if it pacified my father who was
a boy then and who wanted to give her presents. And
it was always tennis shoes because they were the only
kind she would put on and because with her little bit of

38

shuffling around in the sun, she managed to wear out a pair every year. So now that I was doing it, the time would come, and Vesta, who was her daughter and had taken her mother's place and who didn't have much faith in my memory, would look up at me from stringing beans or waxing the floor and say, "Mr. Ed, Mama's feets going to be flat on the ground by next week," and then I would drive out, and it would be her birthday.

My mother goes out very seldom now, so late in the afternoon of the Fourth, I took the shoes and climbed in the broiling car alone and headed down the Embro road where she lived with Vesta and Vesta's husband, where she had lived ever since she took up with Uncle Ben Harrison in the Year One and started having those children that had more or less vanished. (My grandfather asked her once just when was it she and Ben got married. She smiled and said, "Mr. Buddy, *you* know we ain't married. We just made arrangements.")

All the way out there the shoulders of the dirt road were full of Negroes dressed up in a lot of light-colored clothes that were getting dustier by the minute, walking nowhere (except maybe to some big baptizing up the creek) slow and happy with a lot of laughing and with children bunched along every now and then, yelling and prancing and important-looking as puppies on the verge of being grown and running away. I waved at several of the struggling knots as I passed just so I could look in the mirror and see the children all stop their scuffling and string out in a line with great wide eyes and all those teeth and watch my car till it was gone, wondering who in the world that waving white man was, flying on by them to the creek.

There was still the creek to cross that I and a little Negro named Walter had dammed up a thousand times for wading purposes. It would follow along on the left, and there would be that solid mile of cool shade and sand and honeysuckle and the two chimneys that had belonged to Lord-knows-what rising from the far end of it and the sawdust pile that had swallowed Harp Hubbard at age eleven so afterwards we couldn't play there except in secret and always had to bathe before going home, and then on the right it would be her place.

About all you could say for her place was it would keep out a gentle rain, balancing on its own low knoll on four rock legs so delicate it seemed she could move once, sitting now tall in her chair on one end of the porch, and send the whole thing—house, dog, flowers, herself, all—turning quietly down past the nodding chickens and the one mulberry tree to the road, if she hadn't been lighter than a fall leaf and nearly as dry. I got out of the car without even waking her dog and started towards her.

She sat there the way she had sat every day for eight years (every day since that evening after supper when she stepped to the living room door and called my father out and asked him, "Mr. Phil, ain't it about time I'm taking me a rest?"), facing whoever might pass and the trees and beyond and gradually not seeing any of them, her hands laid palm up on her knees, her back and her head held straight as any boy and in that black hat nobody ever saw her without but which got changed—by night—every year or so, a little deaf and with no sight at all and her teeth gone and her lips

caved in forever, leaving her nothing but those sad-
dles of bone under her eyes and her age which nobody knew (at times you could make her remember
when General Lee took up my grandmother who was
a baby and kissed her) and her name which my great-
grandfather had been called on to give her and which
came from a book he was reading at the time—
Warrior Princess Ozimba.

I climbed the steps till I stood directly in front of
her, level with her shut eyes and blocking the late sun
which had made her this year the same as every year
the color of bright old pennies that made us all pretend
she was an Indian when we were children and spy on
her from behind doors and think she knew things she
wasn't telling. I wasn't sure she was awake until she
said, "Good evening to you," and I said, "Good evening, Aunt Zimby. How are you getting on?"

"Mighty well for an old woman," she said, "with all
this good-feeling sunshine."

"Yes, it *is* good weather," I said. "We'll be calling
for a little rain soon though."

"Maybe you all will," she said, "but it's the sun and
not the rain that helps my misery. And if you just step
out of my light, please sir, I can take the last of it." So
I sat down on the top step by her feet that were in
what was left of last year's shoes, and the sun spread
back over her face, and whatever it was my great-
grandfather thought the Warrior Princess Ozimba
looked like, it must have been something like that.

When she spoke again it seemed to confirm she
knew somebody was with her. "I been setting here
wondering is my mulberries ripe yet?"

I looked down at her knobby little tree and said "No, not yet."

"My white folks that I works for, they littlest boy named Phil, and he do love the mulberries. One day his Mama was going off somewhere, and she say to him, 'Phil, don't you eat n'er one of them mulberries.' So he say, 'No ma'm' like he swearing in court. Well, I give him his dinner, and he go streaking off down the back of the lot. That afternoon I setting on the kitchen steps, resting my feets, and Phil he come up towards me through the yard, no bigger than a mosquito, and ask me, 'Aunt Zimby, what you studying about?' I say to him I just wondering if them mulberries back yonder is fit to eat yet. And he don't do nothing but stand there and turn up that face of his, round as a dollar watch and just as solemn but with the mulberry juice ringing round his mouth bright as any wreath, and he say, 'I expect they is.'"

I thought she was going to laugh—I did, softly— but suddenly she was still as before, and then a smile broke out on her mouth as if it had taken that long for the story to work from her lips into her mind, and when the smile was dying off, she jerked her hand that was almost a great brown bird's wing paddling the air once across her eyes. It was the first time she had moved, and coming quick as it did, it made me think for a minute she had opened her eyes with her hand and would be turning now to see who I was. But the one move was all, and she was back in her age like sleep so deep and still I couldn't have sworn she was breathing even, if there hadn't been the last of the sun on her face and the color streaming under the skin.

I sat for a while, not thinking of anything except

that it was cooling off and that I would count to a hundred and leave if she hadn't moved or spoken. I counted and it seemed she wasn't coming back from wherever she was, not today, so I set the shoe box by the side of her chair and got up to go. Vesta would see them when she came at dark to lead her mother in. I was all the way down the steps, going slow, hoping the dog wouldn't bark, when she spoke, "You don't know my Mr. Phil, does you?"

I walked back so she could hear me and said No, I didn't believe I did. There was no use confusing her now and starting her to remembering my father and maybe crying. Nobody had told her when he died.

She felt for the tin can beside her chair and turned away from me and spat her snuff into it. (She had said before that if she was going sinning on to her grave after dips of snuff, it was her own business, but she wasn't asking nobody else to watch her doing it.) Those few slow moves as gentle and breakable as some long-necked waterfowl brought her to life again, and when she had set her can down, I thought I ought to say something so I got back onto how nice the weather was.

But she held her eyes shut, knowing maybe that if she had opened them and hadn't been blind anyhow, she would have seen I wasn't who she had expected all year long. "Yes sir, this here's the weather you all wants for your dances, ain't it?"

I said, "Yes, it would be ideal for that."

"Well, is you been dancing much lately, Mr. Phil?"

She seemed to think she was talking to me so I said No, there wasn't much of that going on these days.

"You a great one for the dancing, ain't you, Mr.

Phil?" All I did was laugh loud enough for her to hear me, but she wiped her mouth with a small yellow rag, and I could see that—not meaning to, not meaning to at all—I had started her.

She began with a short laugh of her own and drummed out a noiseless tune on the arm of the chair and nodded her head and said, "You *is* a case, Mr. Phil."

I asked her what did she mean because I couldn't leave now.

"I was just thinking about that evening you went off to some dance with one of your missy-girls, you in your white trousers looking like snow was on the way. And late that night I was out there on you all's back porch, and it come up a rain, and directly you come strolling up with not a thing on but your underwear and your feets in them white shoes you was putting down like stove lids, and there was your white trousers laid pretty as you please over your arm to keep from getting them muddy. Does you remember that, Mr. Phil?"

I said there were right many things I didn't remember these days.

"The same with me," she said, "except every once in a while . . ." A line of black children passed up the road. They every one of them looked towards us and then towards the older tall yellow girl who led the line and who had been silently deputized to wave and say, "How you this evening, Miss Zimby?"—not looking for an answer surely, not even looking to be heard, just in respect as when you speak to the sea. ". . . What put me to thinking about Mr. Phil is it's time for me some new shoes."

And there I was with the shoes in my hands that I couldn't give her now and wondering what I could do, and while I was wondering she raised her own long foot and stamped the floor three times, and there was considerable noise, as surprising as if that same bird she kept reminding me of had beat the air with its foot and made thunder. Before I could guess why she had done it, Vesta came to the front door and said, "Lord, Mr. Ed, I didn't know you was out here. Me and Lonnie was in yonder lying down, and I just figured it was Mama going on to herself." Then she said louder to Aunt Zimby, "What you call me for, Mama?"

It took her a little while to remember. "Vesta, when have Mr. Phil been here? It ain't been long is it?"

Vesta looked at me for an answer but I was no help. "No Mama, it ain't been so long."

"He ain't sick or nothing is he? Because it's getting time for me some new shoes."

"It won't be long, Mama. Mr. Phil ain't never forgot you yet."

And that seemed to settle it for her. The little tune she had been thumping out slowed down and stopped, and next her head began to nod, all as quick as if she had worked the whole day out in the cotton and come home and fixed everybody's supper and seen them to bed and pressed a shirt for Uncle Ben who drove a taxi occasionally and then fallen dead to sleep in the sounding dark with the others breathing all round her.

Vesta and I stayed still by her till we could hear breathing, but when it began, small and slow, I handed Vesta the shoes. She knew and smiled and nodded, and I told her to go in and let her mother sleep. I stood there those last few minutes, looking through sudden

amazed tears at all that age and remembering my dead
father.

Evening was coming on but the heat was everywhere still. I took the steps slowly down, and as I expected the old dog came up, and I waited while he
decided what to do about me. Over the sounds of his
smelling there came a crowd of high rushing nameless
notes and her voice among them, low and quiet and
firm on the air, "*You* can see them little birds can't
you, Mr. Phil? I used to take a joy watching them little
fellows playing before they went to sleep."

I knew it would be wrong to answer now, but I
looked without a word to where her open eyes rested
across the road to the darkening field and the two
chimneys, and yes, they were there, going off against
the evening like out of pistols, hard dark bullets that
arched dark on the sky and curled and showered to the
sturdy trees beneath.

MICHAEL
EGERTON

H E WAS THE FIRST BOY I MET AT CAMP. HE
had got there before me, and he and a man
were taking things out of a suitcase when I
walked into the cabin. He came over and started talking right away without even knowing me. He even
shook hands. I don't think I had ever shaken hands
with anyone my own age before. Not that I minded. I
was just surprised and had to find a place to put my
duffel bag before I could give him my hand. His name
was Michael, Michael Egerton. He was taller than I
was, and although it was only June, he already had the
sort of suntan that would leave his hair white all summer. I knew he couldn't be more than twelve. I
wouldn't be twelve until February. If you were twelve
you usually had to go to one of the senior cabins across

the hill. But his face was old because of the bones under his eyes that showed through the skin.

He introduced me to the man. It was his father but they didn't look alike. His father was a newspaperman and the suitcase they were unpacking had stickers on it that said Rome and Paris, London and Bombay. His father said he would be going back to Europe soon to report about the Army and that Michael would be settled here in camp for a while. I was to keep on eye on Mike, he said, and if he got to France in time, he would try to send us something. He said he could tell that Mike and I were going to be great friends and that I might want to go with Mike to his aunt's when camp was over. I might like to see where Old Mike would be living from now on. It was a beautiful place, he said. I could tell he was getting ready to leave. He had seen Michael make up his bed and fill the locker with clothes, and he was beginning to talk the way everybody does when they are leaving somewhere—loud and with a lot of laughing.

He took Michael over to a corner, and I started unpacking my bag. I could see them though and he gave Michael some money, and they talked about how much Michael was going to enjoy the summer and how much bigger he would be when his father got back and how he was to think of his aunt just like his mother. Then Michael reached up and kissed his father. He didn't seem at all embarrassed to do it. They walked back towards me and in a voice louder than before, Mr. Egerton told me again to keep an eye on Old Mike— not that he would need it but it wouldn't hurt. That was a little funny since Michael was so much bigger than I was, but anyway I said I would because that was

what I was supposed to say. And then he left. He said
there wouldn't be any need for Mike to walk with him
to the car, but Michael wanted to so I watched them
walk down the hill together. They stood by the car for
a minute, and then Michael kissed him again right in
front of all those boys and parents and counselors. Michael stood there until his father's car had passed
through the camp gate. He waved once. Then he came
on back up the hill.

ALL EIGHT OF THE BOYS IN OUR CABIN WENT TO THE
dining hall together that night, but afterward at campfire Michael and I sat a little way off from the others
and talked softly while they sang. He talked some
about his father and how he was one of the best war
correspondents in the business. It wasn't like bragging
because he asked me about my father and what my
mother was like. I started to ask him about his mother,
but I remembered that he hadn't said anything about
her, and I thought she might be dead. But in a while he
said very matter-of-factly that his mother didn't live
with him and his father, hadn't lived with them for
almost a year. That was all. He hadn't seen his mother
for a year. He didn't say whether she was sick or what,
and I wasn't going to ask.

For a long time after that we didn't say anything.
We were sitting on a mound at the foot of a tree just
high enough to look down on the other boys around
the fire. They were all red in the light, and those fur-
thest from the blaze huddled together and drew their
heads down because the nights in the mountains were
cold, even in June. They had started singing a song
that I didn't know. It was called "Green Grow the

Rushes." But Michael knew it and sang and I listened to him. It was almost like church with one person singing against a large soft choir. At the end the camp director stood up and made a speech about this was going to be the best season in the history of Redwood which was the finest camp in the land as it was bound to be with as fine a group of boys and counselors as he had sitting right here in front of him. He said it would be a perfect summer if everybody would practice the Golden Rule twenty-four hours a day and treat everybody like we wanted to be treated—like real men.

When we got back to the cabin, the other boys were already running around in the lantern light naked and slapping each other's behinds with wet towels. But soon the counselor blew the light out, and we got in bed in the dark. Michael was in the bunk over me. We had sentence prayers. Michael asked God to bless his father when he got to France. One boy named Robin Mickle who was a Catholic said a Hail Mary. It surprised most of the others. Some of them even laughed as if he was telling a joke. Everything quieted down though and we were half asleep when somebody started blowing Taps on a bugle. It woke us all up and we waited in the dark for it to stop so we could sleep.

MICHAEL TURNED OUT TO BE MY BEST FRIEND. Every morning after breakfast everybody was supposed to lie on their beds quietly for Thought Time and think about the Bible, but Michael and I would sit on my bed and talk. I told Michael a lot of things I had never told anyone else. I don't know why I told him. I just wanted him to know everything there was to know about me. It was a long time before I realized that I didn't know much about Michael except what I could see—that he didn't live with his mother and his father was a great war correspondent who was probably back in France now. He just wasn't the kind to tell you a lot. He would listen to everything you had to say as if he wanted to hear it and was glad you wanted to tell him. But then he would change the subject and start talking about baseball or something. He was a very good baseball player, the best on the junior cabin team. Every boy in our cabin was on the team, and it looked as if with Michael pitching we might take the junior title for the Colossians. That was the name of our team. All the athletic teams in camp were named for one of the letters that St. Paul wrote. We practiced every afternoon after rest period, but first we went to the Main Lodge for mail. I got a letter almost every day, and Michael had got two or three from his aunt, but it wasn't until almost three weeks passed that he got the airmail letter from France. There weren't any pictures or souvenirs in it, but I don't suppose Mr. Egerton had too much time for that. He did mention me though I could tell by the way he wrote that he didn't remember my name. Still it was very nice to be thought of by a famous war correspondent. Michael said we could write him a letter together soon and that he would ask his father for a picture.

WE WROTE HIM TWICE BUT FOUR WEEKS PASSED AND nothing else came, not from France. I had any number of letters myself and the legal limit of boxes (which was one a week) that I wanted to share with just Michael but had to share with everybody. Robin Mickle included. Worse than sharing, I dreaded my boxes because I kept thinking they would make me homesick, but with Michael and all the things to do, they never bothered me, and before I expected it, there was only a week of camp left and we would go home. That was why we were playing the semifinals that day—so the winners could be recognized at the Farewell Banquet on the last night of camp. The Colossians were going to play the Ephesians after rest period. We were all in the cabin trying to rest, but everybody was too excited, everybody except Michael who was almost asleep when the camp director walked in and said that Michael Egerton was to go down to the Lodge porch right away as he had visitors. Michael got up and combed his hair, and just before he left he told everybody he would see them at the game and that we were going to win.

The Lodge wasn't too far from our cabin, and I could see him walking down there. A car was parked by the porch. Michael got pretty close to it. Then he stopped. I thought he had forgotten something and was coming back to the cabin, but the car doors opened and a man and a woman got out. I knew it was his mother. He couldn't have looked any more like her. She bent over and kissed him. Then she must have introduced him to the man. She said something and the man stepped up and shook Michael's hand. They started talking. I couldn't hear them and since they weren't doing anything I lay back down and read for a while. Rest period was almost over when I looked again. The car was gone and there was no one in front of the Lodge. It was time for the semifinals, and Michael hadn't showed up. Robin, who was in charge of the Colossians, told me to get Michael wherever he was, and I looked all over camp. He just wasn't there. I didn't have time to go up in the woods behind the cabins, but I yelled and there was no answer. So I had to give up because the game was waiting. Michael never came. A little fat boy named Billy Joe Moffitt took his place and we lost. Everybody wondered what had happened to Michael. I was sure he hadn't left camp with his mother because he would have told somebody first so after the game I ran back ahead of the others. Michael wasn't on his bed. I walked through the hall and opened the bathroom door. He was standing at the window with his back to me. "Mike, why in the world didn't you play?"

He didn't even turn around.

"We lost, Mike."

He just stood there tying little knots in the shade cord. When the others came in from the game, I met them at the door. I told them Michael was sick.

BUT HE WENT TO THE CAMPFIRE WITH ME THAT night. He didn't say much and I didn't know what to ask him. "Was that your mother this afternoon?"

"Yes."

"What was she doing up here?"

"On a vacation or something."

I don't guess I should have asked him but I did. "Who was that with her?"

"Some man. I don't know. Just some man."

It was like every night. We were sitting in our place by the tree. The others were singing and we were listening. Then he started talking very fast.

"My mother said, 'Michael, this is your new father. How do you like having two fathers?'"

Before I could think what to say, he said he was cold
and got up and walked back to the cabin. I didn't follow him. I didn't even ask him if he was feeling all
right. When I got to the cabin, he was in bed pretend-
ing to be asleep, but long after Taps I could hear him
turning. I tried to stay awake until he went to sleep.
Once I sat up and started to reach out and touch him
but I didn't. I was very tired.

ALL THAT WAS A WEEK BEFORE THE END OF CAMP.
The boys in our cabin started talking about him. He
had stopped playing ball. He wouldn't swim in the
camp meet. He didn't even go on the Sunday hike up
to Johnson's Knob. He sat on his bed with his clothes
on most of the time. They never did anything nice for
him. They were always doing things like tying his
shoelaces together. It was no use trying to stop them.
All they knew was that Michael Egerton had screwed
their chance to be camp baseball champions. They
didn't want to know the reason, not even the counselor. And I wasn't going to tell them. They even
poured water on his mattress one night and laughed
the whole next day about Michael wetting the bed.

The day before we left camp, the counselors voted
on a Camp Spirit Cabin. They had kept some sort of
record of our activities and athletic events. The cabin
with the most Good Camper points usually won. We
didn't win. Robin and the others told Michael that he
made us lose because he never did anything. They told
everybody that Michael Egerton made our cabin lose.

That night we were bathing and getting dressed for
the Farewell Banquet. Nobody had expected Michael
to go, but without saying anything he started getting

dressed. Someone noticed him and said something about Mr. Michael honoring us with his presence at dinner. He had finished dressing when four of the boys took him and tied him between two bunks with his arms stretched out. He didn't fight. He let them treat him like some animal, and he looked as if he was crucified. Then they went to the banquet and left him tied there. I went with them but while they were laughing about hamstringing that damned Michael, I slipped away and went back to untie him. When I got there he had already got loose. I knew he was in the bathroom. I could hear him. I walked to the door and whispered "Mike, it's me." I don't think he heard me. I started to open the door but I didn't. I walked back out and down the hill to the dining hall. They even had the porch lights on, and they had already started singing.

THE ANNIVERSARY

ALL THAT WEEK EVERY TIME MISS LILLIAN Belle got still and cool, she knew she was waiting for something, the way little leathery country boys wait on their porches in the evening, not knowing what for, their work done, holding their knees and looking out towards darkness and the road. But it didn't worry her. It would come in a little (something she had forgot that was already gone or something that was coming), and if she never remembered, well, she was seventy-two years old, and she couldn't get herself upset every time her memory failed, and anyhow she had work to do—her Brother's meals to cook. Betty their cook was out of the kitchen for the fifth straight day, grieving for Henry her husband, holding him out of the ground that whole rainy week to bury him right, in sunshine, and everybody knew Lillian Belle Carraway couldn't make a thing but

mints. Still, she did her best. She forced herself
through the suffocating heat, and all that happened to
remind her of what was forgotten didn't remind her at
all, not even the dove mourning by night in the sil-
vered eaves of the house or Brother's dogs with all
their barking at the moon or Pretty Billy's mustache
cup she had dusted twice already that week without
seeing any more than if she hadn't painted them there
herself, forty-five years ago, the plain gold flowers and
the words she had chosen then with such shy care,
"Forget Me Not, Forget Me Never." And it might
have gone on that way another week or longer—those
pieces of the past riding by her no more noticed than
old cars on the public road—if Brother hadn't said at
dinner, "How are you holding up under this heat?"
(His voice was cool and faraway as a medical doctor's.)

She told him, "Brother, I am not as strong as I
look." And she wasn't, though sitting there under
those grand cheekbones, round, high and pure white
as china doorknobs, and her thick hair black as night
still, she looked for all the world firm and impassable
as a good privet hedge. ("The Indian blood," Papa
used to tell her and laugh—"Very little, to be sure,
and what there is from Pocahontas.") But strong or
weak, how could she say what she had thought all
morning?—that she had no business at Henry Twitty's
funeral in the heat—when everybody knew she and
Brother still owed Henry that great debt of thanks
which dying didn't cancel for being the Negro of all
they knew who offered to chauffeur their father in the
very last days when his blood rose higher than science
could record and all that would cool him off was to
send for Henry, day or night, and say, "Take Papa to

ride" and watch them sail off into the wind at sixty miles an hour, glasses rolled down and Papa like a statue on the seat till he felt relief and when that came, saying, "Much obliged, Henry. I'm much obliged"? Facing such a debt, how could she say "I'm staying home"? Letting Henry down, even now, would be like letting Papa down, and she couldn't do that of her own free will.

So Brother did it for her. He laid down his knife and fork and said, "You stay at home. Every Negro on the place will be there and every Elk from Warrenton." He took out the silver toothpick, and they were both quiet a minute. (He was right about the Elks. Henry was something big in the Elks and died dead-drunk on his own front porch. He had often told Betty never to let him lie down drunk or else his heart would float, but she didn't get home that evening till late and it had floated.) Then Brother stood and said, "Betty won't miss you in the crowd."

"That's a lie," she said. "You know there's a pew waiting empty for nothing but two Carraways."

He said, "I'm one Carraway and that's what they'll get today. You stay home and rest." He stepped to the porch and sat awhile, and she went back to the kitchen to finish there. When it came time to go, Brother walked through the hall and said "Goodbye" and went to the funeral, not letting her speak a word. She watched him awhile out the open kitchen window, pulling at her fingers, drawing the blood, slow and violet, back into them, standing that way till the dust of his truck had settled. Then she turned towards the parlor for the first time in months as it would be cool in there.

She sat and thought about fixing Brother's supper, rocking on Mama's green velvet carpet easy as if Mama herself was there in the door, looking long and saying, "Lillian Belle, would you tell me what you think this is? Sunday? You'll cut through to China in less than an hour that way." (One time she had answered, "Mama, me and Brother will just move to the Thorntons'. They let you rock till you're blue in the face and slam doors!") The air of the parlor felt her all over like the coolest kind of hand, and when she caught her head bobbing foolish as a hen's, she said out loud, "If I'm going to sleep I might as well give up now and go to the bed and stretch out." She stood and walked to the mantel where her glasses were. She always laid them there when she rocked. Rocking in her glasses made her dizzy. She put them on and looked up to get them adjusted. And there it was, hanging a little too high and almost out of her sight now but familiar and stinging still. Remembrance took her from her head down to every part the way a breeze will take itself straight down the hall of a house when you had almost given up hope for it, cooling every room as it goes.

Not moved once and barely dusted since Papa had it made for her up in Petersburg and it came down through the mail without even breaking the glass. A splendid likeness of Pretty Billy—eyes faded a little but still so deep in his head it seemed you could never come near them, not if you set out this minute and walked in that direction towards him, not eating or drinking till you dropped. And who in the world, was the first thing she always wondered when she saw it, had ever kept him still that long? And wasn't it funny after all? (though she never thought that till Papa died)—Pretty Billy Williams set there in a border of black with doves in gentle flight around him, thin white streamers in their crossed pink mouths falling over his head after so much time, curling in and out of the poem.

> *Death our dearest ties can sever,*
> *Take our loved ones from our side,*
> *Bear them from our homes forever*
> *O'er the dark cold river's tide.*
>
> *In that happy land we'll meet them,*
> *With those loved and gone before,*
> *And again with joy we'll greet them*
> *There where parting is no more.*

"All the time," she said, "that was what it was." And she would have touched the frame to straighten it if it hadn't stained itself in that one place Papa gave it all those years ago.

SHE CAME OUT ON THE BACK PORCH AND SHADED her eyes and tried to see down that way. She had missed getting the proper eyes, the Carraway eyes to go with the face, and the ones she had, narrow and dun, could only make out the large things now that hung on the sky flat and swaying as clothes on a line— the perfectly round oak tree people still drove miles to look at and where Aunt Dorcas Simpson's place had gone, leaving its chimney alone and old already as Aunt Dorcas was at death and getting older, and Liney Twitty's place huddled to the ground, cowed-looking and yet, you knew, as strong as a hound dog when you call his name and make him come. All the other things that belonged there were gone. At least to her eyes, and from here.

She took down her yard hat and put it on—lacquered black straw with plaster fruit like bullets on the brim—and in her right hand were flowers from the vase in the hall. She went down the steps to the yard, taking each step careful as some altogether new place, and began her walking by a fence that traveled in curves far as anyone could see, walking her age gently but worriedly the way an old mother dog must walk straddling gray and swollen dugs, and the white dirt powdered under her feet and sifted away in the occasional breeze. (It was dry already from the rain.) Then she came to where the dirt was hard and packed. That was Liney Twitty's yard, swept by brush brooms till it shone like Liney's own ivory hand. Any other day she would have gone in and sat awhile with Liney who was her own age, but Liney to be sure had a front seat at the funeral. She slacked up to rest just the same, and what had looked like a black fence post turned into General Washington standing by a chinaberry tree, breaking waxy berries with a dusty toe. He was Liney's grandchild who lived with her.

Miss Lillian Belle said, "Good afternoon, Wash. What in the world are you doing in the broiling sun—frying your brains?"

"Nothing," he said, "but waiting till the funeral lets out."

"Well, come on then and help me do what I've got to do."

"What you got to do, Miss Lillian Belle?"

"I've got to go to the graves. Three days ago was Mr. Pretty Billy's anniversary and I forgot."

GOING TO THE GRAVES THEY PASSED WHERE THE first house had been, the one Mr. Idle Carraway her grandfather had built and called Antaeus Hill (because its earth sustained him) till his wife changed it to Roman Hill (because nobody but Idle, she said, had ever heard of Antaeus before). Miss Lillian Belle told people who asked that she never saw Old Roman Hill "in person" because it burned from lightning while Mr. Idle was in Mississippi with his wife and children, selling race horses which all the Carraways raised back then. Somebody sent him the news and right away he telegraphed a poem to the Raleigh paper, and they printed it on Easter Monday. Every Carraway since got to know the poem by heart, including children, as Mr. Idle sent it in to the paper every anniversary of the fire until he died, and Miss Lillian Belle and Brother and all kinds of little Negroes used to climb in the old black bones of the house, dodging flaming clusters of cow itch and screaming their grandfather's poem so loud that lizards broke off their tails in fright and scattered for the dark.

> March 12, 18—
> *The Hand of God did cloud the day*
> *To chasten Idle Carraway,*
> *For out the Blue a sizzling blast*
> *Hath laid to waste a Proud Man's past*
> *And all his hope to build on land*
> *A mansion that would ever stand*

To give sweet witness to his name
And sent through Carolin' his fame . . .

They passed on by it in no time now, even walking slow as Miss Lillian Belle did with Wash spinning and flinging himself like a limber dishrag. He went by without looking once—just turned up to Miss Lillian Belle and said, "Big Mama have seen right smart dead peoples over there," and because she hadn't been there in over a year and because she had to stop to catch her breath, Miss Lillian Belle looked to where a few bricks and a beam or two were wrapped in yards of honeysuckle, and what she thought of was the nine upright beams that stood there through her childhood —to yell the poem to—till the Negroes commenced cutting at them by night for kindling, cutting at the base of each beam till all nine stood like pencils some-body was trimming patiently year by year. After that they fell too and were dragged away by whoever wanted them and used for things Mr. Idle Carraway, who was a strong man, would have wept to see.

She turned back to say to Wash, "I expect she has, Wash. I expect she has," but she said it to herself— Wash had flung to the end of the path and opened the wrought-iron gate. She couldn't see him but his high voice came to her through the heavy air, "Here he, Miss Lillian Belle. Here he be."

THERE WERE EIGHTEEN GRAVES, SEVENTEEN OF them Carraways who had died—the biggest number in bed back in the house—knowing this was where they would come. (One or two had been shipped in—one boy from Shiloh and one they knew very little about, a distant cousin from Walkerton that just turned up one day, boxed, in the Express Office.) And inside the fence there was periwinkle crawling everywhere to set the place off from the field all around and the rows of tobacco that came to the fence in order and stopped. With all that greenery you couldn't say where one grave stopped and the next one began, but they were there—all of them—the way they knew they would be, together. Miss Lillian Belle's Papa had lived long enough to plan it right, long enough to see that Lillian Belle and Brother were the last, and when their mother took the next-to-last place in the old plot and Brother suggested maybe they could buy a little piece for him and Lillian Belle in the church cemetery, Papa opened the fence and took in a few more yards of field and said, "I had just as soon you were buried upright in the State Museum as in a public graveyard where the ones that cut the grass over your head don't know any more about you than what can be got on a tombstone" which in Papa's case was

J. B. CARRAWAY

A BAPTIST   A DEMOCRAT

But Wash stood on another grave, square and still for the first time on the one place that wasn't a Carraway, with his feet hid deep in the vine and his legs growing up like narrow black trees to the mouth that kept singing, "Here Mr. Pretty Bill, here he, Miss Lillian Belle!" to the dry little tune he patted with his hand on the stone that said in small letters, WILLIAM WILLIAMS—A FRIEND.

THE PLACE WAS IN FULL SUN SO UNDER HER BROAD-brimmed hat, Miss Lillian Belle stood in the gate while her head and her eyes finished swimming, and to stop Wash's singing she said, "What do you know about him?"

"Big Mama tell me things about him," he said.

Then she saw things plainer and went towards the grave. There was one fruit jar by the stone, half-full of rusty-looking rainwater. She bent over and put in the flowers, and the white skin of her breast fell down on itself in a host of involved wrinkles like a handful of crepe myrtle laid in there, and Wash said, "They won't last ten minutes in that."

She straightened up and studied them. "No, I don't reckon they will."

But Wash was back to the question she asked. "I know about them dogs," he said, "and him getting his neck broke." Then he danced off the grave and fell down in the periwinkle and said to himself, "I'm the onliest Nigger I know who ain't scared of snakes."

Miss Lillian Belle had given up trying to follow him with her eyes. She said, "You didn't ever see him did you?"—and laughed at her own foolishness.

Wash didn't answer right away but in a little he said, "Did he have red hair?"

"No, black as ink."

"I ain't seen him then." And again he waited—what he was thinking was his own business, but what he finally said was, "How old he now, Miss Lillian Belle?"

"That would take more figuring than I care to do," she said. There was a long minute while she looked round to confirm she was there at last before she took her seat sideways and slow on Pretty Billy's stone. "All I can say right off is *I* was twenty-six when he came down here for the first time to Mary Jane McNeill's wedding. Her name was just Mary. I was the one added on the Jane. And that made me the last one of my friends to be single. Papa was beginning to fidget about it, had been for several years so when this very fine-looking young man turned up the week before the wedding to be Best Man, Papa sat up and took notice right away. He was introduced to all as Mr. William Williams from Hamlet who was a telegrapher with the Seaboard Railroad, but Mary Jane and I called him by the name he offered us and then blushed—Pretty Billy. No need to blush. He *was* the prettiest-looking boy I think I ever saw—because that's what he was, a boy. When your Big Mama took her first look at him, Wash, she said, 'That gentleman must be a policeman to look all *that* fine in his something-to-wear.' (Don't ask me where she had seen a policeman before.) The wedding week was a right active one—the McNeills had money if nothing else—and Mary Jane paired me and Pretty Billy off together for several of the functions. At the candy pull he tried to teach me some of the Morse Code. I could see right away that it required speed which I have never had, but I let him go on all evening because of the way he kept taking my finger in his hand—he had a surgeon's hands, that fine and narrow with nothing but a plain gold ring. Well, he kept taking my finger and saying, 'Guess what this means' and tapping out a message on the table and when I asked him what it was he had made me say, just smiling back behind his eyes and not telling me. The wedding was a big success, and Pretty Billy and I carried Mary Jane and her husband to Norlina to take the train for the wedding trip to Washington. I know it was the coldest night of the fall—it was November—and I believe I still had on my Maid of Honor dress (though all I can really remember is I wore a hat with ragged robins on it) so with the wind whipping through the curtains of the car, I was frozen to a polka dot in five minutes and sat there with every pore of my skin standing on end like flagpoles. Pretty Billy and I didn't speak a word till we got to the station and barely spoke one on the way home till I said, 'I have always said, just let me get in an automobile and the wind starts blowing' and he laughed. That finished the wedding and there wasn't anything else to hold him in Macon so he headed back to Hamlet the next day, and I never thought or even hoped, I guess, that I would lay eyes on him again. When Papa asked me what I thought of him, and I said I guessed he was right pleasant, you could see Papa's feathers fall a mile. I don't think I could have cared less. I just went back to my duties— teaching Sunday school and painting china and singing here and there—and every now and then I would go visit Norah Fitts who everybody *knew* was already an old maid. We used to sleep in this high bed of hers and tie our toes together in hopes one of us would forget and get up in the night and drag the other one out on her head. (I have done a number of silly things, but I have generally managed to laugh at myself before

others laughed at me.) Then out of a clear sky comes
this postal card from Hamlet with a picture of the jail
on it—some of Pretty Billy's foolishness—which
struck me as being a little forward at the time as he
asked me to exchange greetings with him, but anyway
the next trip I took into Warrenton, I bought a supply
of cards and sent him one. That went on for weeks.
Papa met every mail train, it looked like to me, and I
had gotten to anticipating them myself. So when summer came Norah and I went down to Augusta for a
month to visit the Bridges sisters, and I got a card
nearly every day I was gone. (Norah said he must be
manufacturing the things.) By the time we started
home, I had so many I almost had to pay Excess Bag-
gage on them. When I got back I pulled out all the
cards, and of course Papa had a fit and so did Mama,
and they bought me an album to keep them in with
mother of pearl all over the cover. I hadn't been home
any time when Pretty Billy wrote a letter at last. (By
that time I had several views of everything in Hamlet.
It's a small place.) He asked me to meet him in Raleigh at the State Fair. Somebody must have told him I
hadn't ever missed a fair in my life—they just couldn't
have one without me—so I wrote and said Yes, I could
meet him, and Mama nearly had a stroke. 'The idea,'
she said, 'of you Lillian Belle traipsing off sixty
miles to Raleigh to meet a very-nearly rank stranger!'
As if she didn't know for a fact he was Mary Jane
McNeill's husband's bosom friend and from good folks
in Moore County though his father and mother were
not living. Well, Mama had put her foot down, and I
was almost resigned when Cousin Florence Russell
heard about it the way she heard about everything—

right out of the empty air—and upped and volunteered to act as chaperone. (Cousin Florence was
every bit as fond of fairs as I was and had been attend-
ing a whole lot longer.) I was humiliated. She looked
like a tomato and belched at the drop of a hat, but she
satisfied Mama so that was that, and we took the
morning excursion train to Raleigh. It was held up I
don't know how long waiting for some Negroes—none
of ours—who had reserved a car to themselves and
then at the last minute didn't turn up because they
couldn't raise the money. I died a thousand deaths the
whole way to Raleigh. I had wired Pretty Billy when I
would meet him, and here we were going to be hours
late, and he would more than likely give me out and
leave, and there I would be with Cousin Florence
laughing, because that's exactly what she would have
done, and going back home to tell for the rest of her
life how Lillian Belle and her beau hadn't made con-
nections. Before long though it was clear we were
going to pull into Raleigh almost on time after all. The
engineer was handling the train like it was an express
wagon, and in no time both of us were dizzy as guinea
hens—Cousin Florence a good deal dizzier than me
however, so much so that she suddenly took down the
box of dinner we had brought and said we wouldn't be
needing *that* and handed it to a little big-eyed boy who
had anyhow been looking up at it ever since he
boarded the train like he expected any minute for the
lid to fly off and reveal—pistols! So I sat the rest of
the way in hunger and misery, worrying that I might
not even recognize Pretty Billy, but when we stepped
off the train in this huge burst of steam that wilted me
something awful and just made Cousin Florence red-

der, there he was on the platform with a little derby
hat sitting on his ears and grinning like a possum.
There wasn't any question about not knowing him on
sight. And oh, we had the grandest time at the fair—
took in everything right down to the pigs and managed
to lose Cousin Florence in the prize oil paintings. (She
waited happy for hours in front of 'The Alps Mountains Under Snow' because it cooled her off.)"

Wash said, "Big Mama say I can go to the Littleton
Fair this year, Miss Lillian Belle, if there be anybody
will take me." He was nearly out of sight in the vine,
but you knew he was listening—he was so still a butterfly had lit on his shining forehead and moved there
softly like breathing.

"Well, I hope you can get there," Miss Lillian Belle
said, "but I won't fool you. It can't *touch* the State Fair
with a forty-foot pole. In particular the fireworks.
Pretty Billy wanted me to stay over for the grandstand
fireworks display at midnight, but I had promised
Mama I would be on the eleven o'clock train—and
even that was daring enough to curl half the hair in
Sixpound Township—and of course Cousin Florence
had collapsed long since and was sitting by the foun-
tain eating peanuts (of all things to come to the State
Fair and eat when she had a bushel of them right on
her own back porch). So he saw us to the train, and I
cried off and on all the way to Macon for what Cousin
Florence described as 'an unknown reason.' But it
wasn't so unknown to me or to Papa either who met us
at the train. One look—by lantern light—was all Papa
needed. He knew me like a book. So what happened
after that wasn't much surprise to any of the family
(though it took right many outsiders off guard, and

Cousin Florence went around telling everybody, 'Lillian Belle's got a beau from "off."' I don't know where she thought Hamlet was—Europe?) There commenced a grand exchange of sealed letters between Pretty Billy and me, and Papa talked Mama (without much trouble) into asking him to spend Christmas with us. He accepted post-haste, not having any other place to go, and Mama and old Aunt Dorcas your great-grandmother and Liney turned the house wrong-sideout, washing curtains that froze on the line and generally stirring up dust until they had sent Brother to bed nearly dead with asthma. I took it all right calmly —a lot calmer than Papa liked—and sat in the parlor making a whole series of Christmas presents for Pretty Billy, most of which Mama decided were too intimate. I spent half my time ripping W. W. monograms off of things Mama said just wouldn't do. Finally Papa told me to give him a mustache cup and that's what I did, but I didn't paint the sentiment on it for the longest kind of time after that. It didn't take much imagining to know that being naturally nervous, he would arrive on the wrong train—at least two trains earlier than he had said and so early in fact that he almost caught Mama in her shimmy which you would practically have to get up before day to do. Every once in a while I remember that Christmas as the brightest time we ever had. Pretty Billy couldn't stand the dark so Mama kept enough lamps going to light the Governor's Mansion, and he stayed with us nearly a week. Of course he had presents for every soul on the place. Mine was a gold cross and chain. Aunt Dorcas took one look at it and said, 'That man means business.' Even at Christmas it was quiet here, though nothing like now. Everybody I knew was married and had stopped having parties, and there wasn't much to offer him in the way of entertainment (and there's always been a limit to the time *I* can sit and talk to one person) so he and Papa went off hunting a lot—neither one of them could hunt worth ten cents—and I sat at home mortified for fear Papa was going to force his hand but he didn't. And when all of us saw him off on the train back to Hamlet, him waving and smiling out from under that little mustache, my youngest brother Doc, who died, asked him, 'Are you Lillian Belle's sweetheart?' and he said. 'I hope I am.' And by that time he was, I guess."

"I been asking Big Mama if it ain't time I'm getting *me* some sweethearts," Wash said. His butterfly was gone now.

Miss Lillian Belle gave a little laugh.

"Well, I'm nine years old and, Miss Lillian Belle, when am I going to get any bigger?"

"Time will tell," she said, and because he had rolled on his stomach and laid his face in the periwinkle and started whistling, she asked, "Are you hearing what I'm telling you, Wash?"

"Yes'm," he said without looking up, "you going on about Mr. Pretty Billy, and you say time will tell."

"It will too. It will. There were some claimed I had seen the last of him when he left after Christmas just because he spent so much time hunting and because I didn't fall all over him with love and care. But that's not my nature, never was, and he knew it and honored me for it though he *was* inclined to want to touch people all the time in spite of everything I said. Still he wrote as regular as clockwork, and his letters were just like his talk. You would read them, sitting right by yourself on the porch, and laugh like a nitwit. I suppose my replies encouraged him, and in February he wrote and wanted to know if he could ask Papa for my hand. It certainly wasn't a *new* idea to me, but coming from Pretty Billy towards the end of one of his foolish letters, I nearly had an attack. I slept on it several days and took out his picture and studied it a good many times before I answered to tell him he could. His letter to Papa came in about a week, and if Papa could have run all the way to Hamlet to say Yes, he would have. You would have thought I was a hundred years old. I was just pushing twenty-eight. So it all went very smoothly. Most of our plans were made by mail—setting the date, I mean, and arranging about the honeymoon at Old Point Comfort and deciding where to live in Hamlet (he suggested we stay at the Seaboard Hotel till I got adjusted)—and I only saw him one more time before the wedding week, and that was when he came down for three days at Easter and spent most of his time riding out alone because horses gave Brother asthma and Papa was having his spring rheumatism. I had no intentions of turning it into a tremendous wedding. I was never the bride type anyway so we were going to keep it small—small as Papa would let us with him charging around telling everybody in sight, white or black, and inviting them. We had decided on September the fifteenth in hopes it might be cooler by then and we could decorate the church with the last of the roses and leaves. The ceremony was to have been in the evening. I've always loved the dark. It's so sad. Pretty Billy arrived a week in advance. Papa and Brother met his train and brought him to the house. That was the only time he ever kissed me, saying it was about time for that now, didn't I reckon? There wasn't much entertaining for us and that suited me fine. I had miles of sewing left to do. After breakfast every morning I would step in the parlor and start to work, and Pretty Billy would come trailing after me. It never seemed to dawn on him that I might not want him watching me make my own step-ins and all but I never mentioned it. (He was the nervous type—always had to be poking up the fire or fiddling with something in his hand. Early in our acquaintance he broke the lace-work skirt off a china ballet dancer Mama valued because it was sent to her from some capital, and when I looked up at him holding out the pieces in his hand and making no attempt to hide them, he said, 'See here, Lillian Belle, what I've done, just fiddling with it,' and I said—and laughed—'It seems to me if you are so much of a fiddler, you had better invest in a fiddle before you cause real trouble.') But he never bothered me long, and from the second day after he arrived, he was riding off every morning to hunt by himself. Most of Papa's dogs would follow after him. Mama would pack him some dinner, and we wouldn't see him again until late evening just before supper. I thought I would be seeing enough of him in the future so I never asked him not to go. He never brought any game or anything back with him except some lovely leaves to decorate the church, and once I asked him, 'Pretty Billy, what is it you are after out there all day long?' and he laughed and said, 'Most anything I can scare up.' (Lord knows what he was hunting at that time of year unless it was a breeze or a cool place to lay his head.) Before I could catch my breath good, it was Thursday morning—Saturday was the wedding—

and I was getting more fidgety by the minute. I would jump out of my skin if you halfway looked at me, but Pretty Billy rode off that morning before I even got downstairs. Mama had taken over the sewing because I was so trembly, and I spent the entire day making mints on a marble-top washstand—one of the few things I do well. I looked for Pretty Billy to come in for dinner since it was Thursday and folks were beginning to call but he didn't. And he didn't show up at three o'clock when Preacher Burton came to discuss details so I had all that to handle alone, and I have never been any sort of manager. It was a cool afternoon and bright, and I decided to sit on the back steps and wait for him, but he didn't appear and dark was fast coming on and the chill so I went in, but I couldn't eat a mouthful of supper. Papa and Brother were worried too though they made out like they weren't. 'He's a splendid rider,' Papa would say every few minutes. 'He must have met up with a friend.' Well, of course he was a great talker, but *who*, was what I wanted to know, did he know out there in the middle of nowhere?"

"Big Mama know if you want to ask her," Wash said—but only to the hot air around. Miss Lillian Belle had gone on to tell it before she forgot.

"When he hadn't come by bedtime, I was all to pieces and nobody could begin to think of sleeping. We all sat there and waited and tried to find little tasks to do, little quiet things that wouldn't jar the air, till the only noise left was Mama's needles knitting Pretty Billy a going-away scarf for his long neck, when out of the pitch dark came this high sad voice that was one hound barking at the moon. And off in the woods the others commenced to answer, and they sounded half the world away. Papa rose up and said 'It's my dogs'—like it might have been dragons. All of us knew enough about those dogs' voices to know they hadn't just now wandered in at Pretty Billy's heels. Papa and Brother went out but they couldn't quiet them down. They stayed out there till I thought I would scream, and when they came in it was to get their coats and lanterns and their guns to ride off looking, taking Uncle Smooth with them—your great-granddaddy—on a mule, and all those crying dogs. I sat by the window with a light till way past midnight. Then Mama made me take off my shoes and rest till we heard some news. That wasn't before nearly seven when Uncle Smooth rode up in the yard on Papa's horse and told Mama that Papa said Miss Lillian Belle was to come to where he was right away. I asked him if they had located Mr. Pretty Billy. All he said was 'Yes'm, they did.' I put on my coat and climbed on the horse behind him (we only kept three riding horses then) and didn't say a word till we got to where we were going. I just prayed to myself and Uncle Smooth took us crashing off through the woods. Where we finally stopped was at the Pitchfords'. You don't know them, Wash."

"Yes'm, Big Mama use their name sometime in stories."

"Well, the Pitchfords I'm talking about were farming a piece of Papa's poorest cotton land over beyond the creek bottom. There are some of them back there right now—the sort of folks you will have to knock in the head on Judgment Day. They had a little house very much like Liney's except darker and dirty, and when Uncle Smooth and I flew up in the yard there was nothing in sight but eight or ten peaked-looking children standing in stairsteps by the door staring at me. Papa said many times afterwards that if there had been any way in the world to spare me the shock of walking in like that, he would have done it. But as it was, they had to lay Pretty Billy out on a bed pushed close up to the fireplace, and he was the first thing I laid eyes on when I walked in that house. It didn't help one bit either that after I had stood in the door a long time, he rolled his eyes over towards me as far as he could and tried to smile and said, 'Look here, Lilly, I've messed up your shirt.' He had just recently been calling me Lilly, and the shirt was one I had made for him. Papa was there and what seemed like a hundred of those Pitchfords creeping around and looking at me out of their big squirrel eyes and saying 'Howdy-do, lady.' Brother had gone on the other horse to get a doctor. I didn't ask but Papa volunteered they had found Pretty Billy thrown down beside the creek a little way from the Pitchfords'. After a while old Mrs. Pitchford came up to Papa and said, 'Major Carraway, it's his neck, ain't it?' and Papa said 'I know that.' They offered me a chair by the fire, and I sat there for the rest of the time about four yards from Pretty Billy's head as I reckoned it. I never went a step closer, and when he died he died just that far from me. Brother and the doctor didn't come and didn't come, and nobody knew anything to do for him except Nettie Pitchford—she was their oldest girl, about seventeen—and she stood there by him and mopped off his forehead with cool water and fanned him whenever the flies settled. He looked at her most of the time and nowhere else. Papa said he couldn't turn his head. It looked like

we might be there a long time, and Mrs. Pitchford
came over and asked me if I wouldn't take a glass of
her tomato wine. I said I didn't believe that was what I
needed, and it was then that Pretty Billy called for
Papa. Papa leaned over and Pretty Billy tried to whisper, but in that room there wasn't such a thing as whispering. What he said was, 'Give her something she
wants.' He was looking at Nettie and smiling."

A thin useless cloud passed over the sun, splotching
the graves with shade, and a little breeze commenced
waving round in the tobacco—nothing to get your
hopes up about—but in the brief dark and under the
brim of her hat, Miss Lillian Belle's eyes went on getting brighter. "I've always known Pretty Billy meant
for Papa to reward that girl for hanging over him faith-
ful like she did with water. Then a fly landed on his
nose. He laughed and a thin stream of blood ran out of
the corner of his mouth, and he gave this little last
sound twice—not a word, but like a dove makes,
round and alone, and I couldn't listen to a dove for the
longest kind of time after that. I ought to have cried
right then before it was too late. If somebody had
laughed at me or said, 'Lillian Belle, I'm sorry' or 'Lillian Belle, you will never be asked to bear a heavier
load than this' then I might have broken down like any
woman should. But I didn't see it that way. The only
person that said *anything* was Papa, and all he said
was, 'Lillian Belle, don't let me down.' It just seemed
like he was counting on me to hold up. It was the first
time I had ever been counted on for anything so I held
up. His brother came that same afternoon, short and
scared-looking. Nobody had given him a thought. He
had come to be Best Man. Papa asked him what was

his wish about burying Pretty Billy, and he said he thought it would be the sensible thing to bury him in Macon. That was what Papa had hoped for so he offered Pretty Billy this space here and did every bit of the bathing and shaving and dressing himself, using my one photograph to locate the part in all that damp black hair. When he had finished the laying out, he led me in to say goodbye or whatever I wanted to say. The casket hadn't come yet and Pretty Billy was lying on the bed he generally slept in with one pillow under his head so the edge of his nose and lips and chin and his eyelids were raised up into the light from the window and seemed to be shining from inside. Papa had shaved off part of his mustache by mistake, and what was left wasn't too much like Pretty Billy. The only thing I could think to do was touch his hand once and then leave. But when I stepped forward to do it, I saw how the fingers of his right hand had curled inwards to make a cup like a seashell waiting for water, and I didn't want to disturb that. So I turned to Papa and said 'I'm ready' and he took me away. It was to have been a small wedding, and it was a small burial. Papa stopped our Virginia cousins by wire, and there was just Mama and Papa and Brother and Doc, and the preacher, and Mr. Williams' wife joined him for the service, and little Loyce Rodwell and I, and Nettie Pitchford and her folks turned up but kept their distance. Liney and Aunt Dorcas and Uncle Smooth and some of the others watched from the porch. It was a nice afternoon. Papa had turned the goats loose in the front yard to eat down the tallest weeds, and some little Negro boys had spent that whole morning rolling down all that was left with great big logs. Aunt Dorcas went out a dozen times, I know, and told them to hush up their laughing. Mama had asked Liney to sing a song, and she sang 'Precious Lord, Take My Hand' with no piano or anything, just that clear voice she used to have that carried to the road. Then the men put him on the wagon and brought him down here for the commitment. Loyce Rodwell, who was to have strewn rose petals at the wedding, sprinkled some in over the casket, and Mama and I walked back up to the house. Papa stayed behind, and Brother, to see that the rest was done. Everybody did their best and with time and a mild winter, things had pieced back together nearly when one evening Aunt Dorcas looked out of the kitchen window and said, 'Here come that Pitchford child.' Papa went out to meet her, remembering Pretty Billy's last words that I hadn't ever forgotten. She had walked all that way—four or five miles easily—to ask Papa if as her present she couldn't have that little gold finger ring of Mr. Pretty Billy's. Papa told her it was buried with him, which it was, so she said, 'Well, there ain't nothing else I don't guess' and turned and set off to walk back home in the night."

SHE HAD STOPPED AND SHE SAT ON THE STONE, PICK-ing at any spot on her dress as was her habit. In a little Wash raised up from his greenery—"That's all you re-member, Miss Lillian Belle?"

She nodded. "I'm a mighty good forgetter."

Wash took a small rock and scraped at the moss on the oldest stone Major Carraway had felt compelled to buy for that Walkerton cousin. Miss Lillian Belle stood and looked round her again. It had once been her wish to see the graves from the air because Dorman Spivey had passed over in a plane on his way to war and reported that the Carraway cemetery was the one thing he recognized in all Warren County. Then she said, "Wash, I'll need your hand back up the path," and as if he had been doing it forever, he took her arm and a good part of her weight on his shoulder, and they started—the old woman looking towards where she knew the house was and the little boy studying the ground and leaning into his work with his pink tongue just showing between the dark purple lips.

Soon they would be close enough, and the house would swim into plain view through the heat. Miss Lillian Belle said, "Hold up a minute, Wash, and let me catch my breath," and from there she looked up, but all she could see of it was the silver paint streaking over the eaves and down the east side where Buxton Bragg, a jack-leg roof painter, had spilled it early in the spring. Brother should have seen to that long ago. "I'll speak to him about that this evening," she said, "if I don't forget." Wash was still beside her, plowing little furrows on the dust with his toe and humming. "I'm all right now, Wash. You run on home. Liney and the rest of them will be there directly, and they can tell you about Henry's funeral."

"Yes'm. Then you want me to come tell you, Miss Lillian Belle?"

"Thank you, no, Wash. Brother will be telling me all I can say grace over."

So he said he would be seeing her tomorrow if the Lord was willing and he didn't die, and she moved on towards the house, towards what she could see—the light, that was all, the sun on the spilled paint, the sudden flashing reaching out to her even down here, shining like Christmas all those years ago or like her own old eyes as bright now in remembering as some proud mountain yielding the sun its flanks of snow or some white bird settling its slender wings with the softest cry into dying light.

TROUBLED SLEEP

❖

"HELP" WAS THE FIRST HUMAN THING IT said after cracking down on me unseen and unnamed through the pitch-dark woods and the black honeysuckle and the snakes knee-deep surely on all sides, waiting to be waked up. "Help"—not crying or wanting but announcing calmly as if it knew what I needed most in all the world and was bringing it—to me, Edward Rodwell, nine years old, caught in terror in the August night alone with all around me noises I knew like my own name turned nameless new threats with dark for eyes and damp breaths that raked my bare neck and arms, and all because after supper I played Rummy with my cousin Falcon Rodwell on the porch while the light lasted and lost till I couldn't stand to lose another game and called Falc who was cheating as usual a Cheater, and my father turned round in his chair and said in that case didn't I reckon I ought to go to bed?—but not a word to Falc about wasn't he sorry too and he grinning in hiding behind his solemn face as I marched away to sit in my empty room long as I could with only the sounds from the porch of them joking and remembering and, once, my mother's voice calling out to Falc, "Falc, you look to me like a lighthouse." I leaned out quietly to see what she meant, and she was right— there was Falc charging back and forth in the evening, happy with himself as if I had never been born, reaching out a hand here and there, closing it on the air and adding one more lightning bug to the jar he held, swarmed already with gentle syncopated light. So I slipped out the back and walked the half-mile to this Dark Ring of mine and Falc's in the woods (for burying things and ceremonies) and sat down, thinking of nothing but ways to pay them back and win them back till full night came and caught me in dark close as gloves, and I could only wait, shivering in the heat for whatever would come to take me home where I was remembered no more or for the Devil to leap any minute into the Ring, dancing, or the Old Woman All Skin and bones to lay a pale dry hand rattling on my shoulder and claim me for her own.

But the one word came again—"Help"—held out like a hard pear I could take or leave and, coming closer, sounds like "Who" and "Whoop," and I knew who it was and not seeing how or why, I thought things would get better from now on and that I could let loose the tears locked for fear in my eyes. They streamed down again hot as any acid, and I caught at them with my tongue and swallowed bitterly at the knot rising hard up through my chest and throat, lay-

ing all my misery at the back of my eyes because this
was Falcon Rodwell, my cousin (though I had cause to
wonder why) and my age, who had finally and under
his own steam gone up to the bed we shared all summer and seeing I wasn't there, had known where I was
and had broken through to me for reasons of his own
that he might never tell, asking nobody's permission
and coming in wide lost circles and seeing (and keeping to himself as his cross to bear) who knew how
many things that never got into any book, the things
he always saw the minute the sun went down and the
reasons he never went out after dark without speaking
The Shields nonstop—"Who" and "Help" and whatever else made him breathe out because with his warm
breath, he claimed, came enough germs to hold off
anything the night could offer—but *coming* and towards me, convinced of arriving in time to do what he
had to do and not worried once at being the only thing
on earth to need half an hour to cover the path between our house and this Ring, considering he and I
and Walter Parker (a Negro our age that we blind-
folded sometimes and took with us) had worn a path to
the Ring so deep you could have found your way there
in total eclipse if you had made us tell you there was
such a place, and you couldn't have done that.

So he stumbled into the Ring, not by the one right
ceremonial way but tearing through the round wall of
bushes, breaking every rule we had made, stepping on
the graves of two frogs who died from eating B.B. shot
we gave them, and looking like the night because the
moon wasn't up, black against black trees with only
the pieces of light across his forehead that were the
tails of lightning bugs stuck there still warm and puls-

ing. He stopped ten feet from where I stood and waited for his envelope of germs to clear, resting up for whatever he thought came next.

I wanted to speak to let him know I was there— that I hoped he hadn't come for nothing—thinking if I could make him say one word, I would know why he was here—whether to say my mother had just now passed on unexpectedly in her chair or my father had taken the first drink since the day I was born (when he went out to the woodshed, the only place you couldn't hear my mother screaming—I came feet-first—and fell down and promised to give it up if I lived and I did) or German paratroopers were falling on our house like butterflies or that he was sorry. So "Falc—" I tried and that was it. The knot filled my throat like dry bread.

"Nobody but Falc," he said and started in the direction of his name I had offered, holding out in front of him like somebody blind his arms that changed color as he came the way a crow's wings will in the day— black if he folds them but blue as steel in flight, leaving you glad you noticed him. He came on till his fingers touched my chest. Then slow and straight like an old Indian at a Last Council, he took his seat on the dry ground. I tried to make out the shape of his head but I couldn't yet, except that row of light—maybe it wasn't Falc? But what except Falc smelled like that, like money at the roots of his hair?—so I sat beside him, near as all my doubts and griefs would let me, swallowing hard at my full throat.

How long we stayed that way I don't know—not making a sound and, as if wind was in our hair, our heads rolled back to the round hole in the trees over us that was the sky—but long enough for the stars, which were all the light we had, to begin doing what they normally did when I was that age and sad and looked at them long enough—wheeling down the sky to the left, slow, and when I almost shut my eyes, connecting up in the pictures I saw then wherever I looked—the elephant I prayed regularly to get and Johnny Weissmuller that I wrote letters to, asking if I could be Tarzan when he died, and a lot of people dancing—and the light left over fell down on Falc and me, so bleached and cool that all it touched—our arms and necks and folded legs—was like curved bones you find some days when you are out walking in the woods and bare bones laid neat in the leaves are the last thing you hope to meet.

But that went on in silence so deep my swallowing sounded like rock wrenched out of quarries, and we were so close I could hear Falc's body making its own noises—his slow heart and whatever else was inside him putting up a roar like the sea and the dry sound like feet in sand of a hand rubbing down the calf of his leg—and I kept thinking we would touch, he being all I had, not by reaching out our hands on purpose but maybe by thinking of it till magic took over. It takes two to work that though, and whatever Falc was thinking it wasn't on similar lines so we didn't meet. The only sign he gave of not being dead was—every time he could work one up—a long-range spit through the teeth though my mother had warned him to give up the habit or go hard and dry before his time like Mr. Coley Dickerson, a man we knew who spat in public and was dry as a used whisk broom already, at only middle age.

But I was improving—physically anyhow. My tears and my throat had eased, and that energy went towards making up hurt questions to say, hot and fast, such as "Falcon Rodwell, why in the world—if you are going to be my cousin and spend every summer with me and take what I give—do you do things like tonight?" But I never said it. Ask Falc a question like that, and you'd be in silence up to your ears. He didn't work that way—making up reasons for what he wanted to do. He did it and then if it was a bad idea (and nobody knew in advance what would strike him as a bad idea), he came and sat down where you were, even if it was the bathtub—not speaking or looking at you, but waiting to find his own way out of what he had done, and if that way didn't appear, well, waiting still like a box of Christmas oranges under the tree which if you don't open soon will sit till Doomsday, nailed shut and going bad by the minute.

The trouble was, my terror was gone and with it my joy that those sounds had been Falc's face and name, and I was left with only bitterness that wouldn't let me move—not first—and since moving first was my job, we might have stayed there all night if the sound of a plane hadn't started, out of sight in the back of our heads. We waited for it like our last hope, knowing the chances it had of crossing the hole in our trees were slim, and when we had all but given up, there it was for eight seconds—I counted them, I remember—with red and green lights answering each other back and forth like rhymes, taking soldiers most likely someplace they would rather not go.

So Falc spoke. He had found a way. "Where do you

wish we were?"—meaning to get an answer, trusting I knew what answer to give.

"Dead," I said—the thing I had to say to start his game and the thing I meant, this night.

"Who do you know that's dead?"—meaning me to fill in while he made his plan.

All I could think of were two grandfathers and a grandmother I had never seen and Will Rogers and those frogs and an alligator named Popeye that was sent to me from Florida and lived for two years in my aquarium on lean bacon and was just learning to sing when we got hooked to the city water line with so much chlorine in it, and he stretched out and died. I told him those seven names that were dead, and he said that didn't sound to him such a wonderful group to be so anxious about joining so soon. But that didn't mean for me to stop.

"Where do *you* wish?" I said.

He knew. "Someplace with bears. Like Alaska."

"Yes, and we'd die there in five minutes."

"*You* might but I would go prepared and I would last. I would have a long knife and cut us out a house in the ice and make us a cave to sleep in, and I would peel the skins off of bears for us to wrap up in when the sun went down—except for one bear that I would save named Maurice who would be our friend and stick by us. I would give little birthstone rings and sun shades to every Eskimo we met, and they would come to visit us and drag up whales for us to eat, and I would make a pact with them about how if they did unto us, we would do unto them and vice versa."

"What if we didn't like eating whales?" I said because he was saying "us" and "we" as if he had carried me with him.

"Pemican," he said. "And the Eskimos would take us fishing, and we would divide up what we caught."

"And you would get two times more than anybody else."

"Well, if I did, it would be because I was working two times harder than you and Walter." (So Walter was with us, making it a three-man party. I liked thinking of Walter, black amongst that snow, cool for the first time in his life.) "And if you didn't like it, you could leave. You and Walter would have to go anyhow when winter set in, but I would stay on, making daily broadcasts to the *National Geographic* magazine about what my thermometer said and taking pictures for them, and if you wanted me to, I would play you a record of a song sometimes on Saturday nights and you could listen in. Then one night I would announce I was surrounded by blizzards and how even the Eskimos' blood was freezing fast and how I was alone with the dogs who were lying there staring at me, not bothering to hunt up any rabbits, just waiting for me to go to sleep. But Maurice would be at my side, and if I nodded or took a bath, he would slam off any hungry dog that got ideas—till the germs moved in and everybody started having fever. Finally there wouldn't be anybody left but me, sitting there with Eskimos and dogs dead and frozen all around me and even Maurice stiff as a poker at my side and my flashlight batteries gone, and then I would run out of sulfa medicine, and there wouldn't be anything to do but say The Shields till my throat closed up and I couldn't whisper 'Help!' The germs would know and close in by dripping from the ceiling onto my face and grabbing hold of my fur suit and holding me so I couldn't reach the radio to SOS or even make my will, and nobody would ever hear of me again."

He had told me that story, or one similar, a hundred times, and he always went that way—alone as Custer, staving off every natural foe for days, giving in to germs because you couldn't *see* germs. When we played cowboys, everybody else who had to die died of bullets or arrows, but Falc never died of anything but blood poison or brain fever or milk leg and even then only after he had called me over to where he lay and whispered his Last Will and Testament, leaving me his radio (the only one we knew of that you could get Hitler on, twenty-four hours a day) and making me give my oath to bury him in a copper casket and go to Sunday school and church weekly and turn into a great scientist and destroy germs. I would cry and offer to go with him if he would let me, but it would be too late, and presently he would stop whispering and lower that curtain he kept at the back of his eyes, and I would fall on his chest and listen for his heart (not knowing what a heart sounded like), thinking to myself, "No radio on earth will ever be what Falcon Rodwell was to me."

But no matter about me—Falc had finished his dying and sat quiet—not from sadness but as if the story was a grand bird he had made out of nothing, and when it breathed and spread its wings, there was nothing left but to sit back and maybe smile and watch it take off and circle and sail out of sight forever. Then he cheered up and said, "I am going home now"—not seeing he had left me worse than ever with his sad cold journey and his cheating and my father not trying to understand and the dark laid on me heavier than ice or what I knew about death.

He unfolded his legs and stood and waited. I was supposed to go first, but I sat still and "Falcon," I said, "we have got to lie down now and die in real life." I didn't know what he would say, only that I could count on him not to say "Why?"—the thing anybody else would want to know. Falc knew.

"How?" he said and I thought he was with me, and *how*?, I thought, was the last problem we had, not noticing that my troubles didn't have to be his. All I saw were ways to go for good and take Falc with me.

"Blood Brothers?" I said, having tried two whole summers to make Falc cut his thumb a little and pass a few drops into mine and me into him, but every blade I produced he would look at and say "Not surgical enough" though any number of times he let me go so far as to cut my own thumb before he decided No and left me with blood wasting all over the ground—who knew? maybe the one drop of Indian blood my mother said we had—unless Walter was there to stand in. (After Walter had Brothered with me for the third time, he wanted to know, "When you joining the Niggers, Ed?" And I considered joining.) "Listen, Falc, we would just slice each other's thumbs real easy and lay them together and pass a little back and forth and let the rest run out on the Ring until we went to sleep and didn't wake up, and they would find us in the morning, lying on the bloody Ring, drained-out."

"There's one thing you forgot," he said—there always was—"your personal salvation."

"Oh no, Miss Ellie is in charge of that." (Miss Ellie taught my Sunday school.)

"What makes you so sure Miss Ellie is all that saved herself to go taking on a dozen others?"

"Miss Ellie is a saint."

"Saints don't grow on trees these days, and Miss Ellie wasn't any more baptized than you." (I was going to be a Methodist with my mother, but Falc was from the Baptist part of the Rodwells and knew all about how when Matthew 3:16 said, "And Jesus, when he was baptized, went up straightway out of the water," Matthew meant going *under*, head and foot, otherwise how could you come up out of it?) "So if we walk down to the creek, I'll give you Immersion and take it a second time myself to make sure, and we'll stay under and drown."

I felt that would be going back on my mother and on Miss Ellie who was the only person I knew that wouldn't call John "the Baptist" so I reminded him, "I'm a born floater and you know it."

"Then we could go to a field and start running and run till our hearts popped and we fell out." But Falc could outrun me by miles, and I could see in my mind Falc saying "Go!" and us starting out together and Falc tearing ahead, looking back every now and then, finally seeing me crumple to the ground, and running back and deciding it was his duty now to give up and go home and tell my father. I kept that to myself though, and it looked as if surrender was the one thing left—to feel our way home in our bare feet, knowing one of us was bound to step on a snail before we got there, and take whatever my father decided to give.

But then the moon came up, breaking into our piece of sky, looking the way it ought to look—the way people say it does—and giving us light enough to

read the finest print. I turned and when I had seen
Falc—really seen—for the first time in three hours,
he spoke.

"That's how," he said, pointing up at it.

"How?"

"The moon. The moon will make you crazy."

And it would. Would Walter think of standing in
moonlight? No—if ever he was playing with us after
dark and the moon rose, he would spread his hands
over his head and say, "I don't know about you all, but
I ain't risking the sense I got out in this stuff" and
leave and we wouldn't see Walter till morning. And
didn't everybody know what moonlight did to Tom-
Boy Thompson who got left in it by mistake at the age
of six and rose up next morning turned to a general
embarrassment who collected stray dogs that followed
his bicycle in bony dozens and wore flannel rags
around his neck in the scorching weather without offering a reason and threw cats down garden-house
holes and was six years old every day of his life until he
passed away, as a blessing, by the side of the road to
Wise one evening when everybody was at prayer meeting and only his dogs, wandering into church and sniff-
ing out his mother, told the tale?

"Falc," I said, "we will take off our clothes and
stretch out in it and go to sleep and that will be the end
of us."

"All right," he said—and I thought I had
won—"but what if we don't die?"

"We'll get enough to send us crazy anyhow which
will embarrass Daddy and Mother when they take us
places."

"And I could act like the lady that played tunes to

your Daddy on nothing but the windowsill." (That was something my father had told us from when he was eighteen and took a tour of the State Hospital in Raleigh and got cornered by a very fine-looking lady who said she was North Carolina's finest pipe organist and a pupil of Edward MacDowell and would anybody like for her to prove it? My father said "Yes" and she played "To a Wild Rose" with her long blue fingers— not singing or humming but silent, just on the concrete windowsill that was an organ to her mind. And Falc partly lived for the day when he would be old enough to take the tour and see that lady if she was still alive and ask her to play.)

Then I pulled my sweatshirt over my head for what I reckoned was the last time and unbuckled my pants and thought and decided to leave them on so as to ease the shock on whoever would find us in the morning. I lay back on the cool ground and threw my arms straight back as if I was in water and watched Falc undress exactly that far and lie down too.

"Falc," I said—it was the last thing I ever wanted to know—"what will you miss most?"

"Mosquitoes' singing," he said as if he had settled it years ago for some occasion like this. Then he was quiet. He hadn't wondered once what I would miss.

The moon had turned the Ring around us to the image of the moon, and when we took our places to one side of the center (because nothing ever touched the center but fire and Walter who made the fire), the moon took our bodies, and I thought then we were two narrow boats left together in a silent bloodless world like those that Time Forgot where nothing ever moved or breathed but only quivered in the grip of

that devouring light. Like that—together, I thought—
we waited for sweet avenging death.

But I have never slept well, and before I had
thought of closing my eyes, I could hear Falc's breath
slow down with longer spaces between each sigh till
there was no sighing at all and maybe no breathing. I
said "Falc?" but there was no answer, and I raised up
to see him. His head had turned away from me already, and I leaned over to find his face. Not a breath
of anything came out of him, no more than if I had
been in the valley of the Nile and struck the last blow
at the sealed mouth of some great pharaoh's ancient
grave and had centuries of dry nothing rush out to
meet me. "Falc?" I tried again and took his shoulder
that was hard beneath my hand and cool and shook it.
But Falc had never been too strong on touching people, and I didn't want to touch him now he couldn't
draw back.

Falc had gone ahead as usual and left me here no
better than when the night began and with this body by
me now, cold and stiff as Maurice our bear and those
poor Eskimos, and the moon still pouring down. How
was I to know that once you tried you could go as easy
as that, so easy that your closest friend, one foot away,
couldn't say what breath had been your last or next-to-
last? All I knew was, I had to follow. I owed Falc that
much and where else was there left to go? Again I fell
back and closed my eyes and waited, but I saw things
that wouldn't let *anybody* sleep—me finally dying and
coming to in a golden field that looked happy, with
ripe wheat and trees and a river and rafts full of laughing people and suddenly Falc standing at the front of
the biggest raft by the white sail, talking to the boys all

around him and joking, and every now and then one of them would dive in the water and circle the raft and shout up to Falc a name I had never heard and he would notice them. I ran down to the bank and called out "Falc—" and he turned just his eyes toward the sound of his old name, but they looked straight through me and on past as if I had never come all this way to join him. He turned back and the wind rose and the raft drifted on out of my sight till all I could see was the top of Falc's head by the mast, but that went too and those boys' laughing was the only thing left.

Seeing that, *knowing* that for the first time brought tears I had never wept before, choked out like iron that lay blue and cold on my cheeks and wouldn't fall or dry.

Then Falc stood up alive like fire—from sleep or from a game, I couldn't say—and said, "I am going to pee" and walked straight through the center of the Ring and the ashes towards a low blackjack tree by the edge that we always peed against to kill it, but he walked past that and took the path away. For a long time I could hear him whispering The Shields. They died out though and enough time passed for even Falc to finish, but there wasn't even the sound of him *trying* to come back.

So with all that long day lying on me, I gave up and fell asleep and didn't dream and wasn't dreaming when I felt a hand on the center of my chest. I was too much asleep to jump or shout, but I opened my eyes enough to see it was Falc, come back for his own reasons and feeling for my heart to know if the moon had worked. It hadn't and my heart was beating intolerably like a held bird but Falc didn't know where. For all he could feel and for all I showed him, I was gone beyond recall. He knelt awhile longer. Then he walked around the Ring twice, saying words that sounded old to him and suitable as a service, and I thought he would leave again, but next he was above me with his hands held out—first as if I was fire and he was cold, then with the palms turned up, and whatever olden rite it was to him, it was like giving to me. He stood that way whole minutes, turning every sad color in the moonlight, holding out with both hands what he wasn't ever going to give—his life that I had asked for. Yet thinking I would never know or thank him or ask for more, he found his way. He lay down near me, not too near and in the deadly moon but in half-shade a yard away, and tired as I was, I waited and kept my body quiet till he was asleep. Then I turned towards him and—not knowing what it was like to be Falc—I laid my arm on his chest which was the part of him in the light, and sometime—sleeping, I think—he took my hand.

When they missed us from our bed and my father came out at midnight to lead us home, walking straight as any judge to the bench, he found us in that secret place where he knew we were, and all he could see, he smiled at—me in troubled sleep in the full moon still and Falc dark and gone like he didn't mean to return, but in each other's arms at least and breathing slow.

UNCLE GRANT

S UPPOSING HE COULD KNOW I HAVE THOUGHT
of him all this week. Supposing I was not three
thousand miles from northeast North Carolina
and supposing he had not been dead six years and I
could find him and say, "I have thought of you all this
week"—then he would be happy. Supposing though he
was alive and I was still here in England—in Oxford
whose light and color and trees and even grass would
be strange to him as the moon (as they are to me)—
and supposing he heard I had thought of him. It would
go more or less like this. He would be in my aunt's
kitchen in a straight black chair near the stove, having
finished his breakfast. My aunt would have finished
before he started and by then would be spreading beds
or sweeping the porch, in her nightdress still. So he
would be alone—his natural way, the way he had
spent, say, sixty percent of his life, counting sleep. His

back would be straight as the chair, but his body would lean to the left, resting. The way he rested was to feel out the table beside him with his left elbow (an apple-green table with red oilcloth for a cover) and finding a spot, press down and then lay his head, his *face*, in his hand. His long right arm would lie on his hollow flank, the fingers hinged on the knee, and his legs would be clasped, uncrossed not to wrinkle the starched khaki trousers and ending in high-top shoes that, winter or summer, would be slashed into airy patterns, clean as the day they were bought, just ventilated with a razor blade. His white suspenders would rise from his waist to his shoulders, crossing the starched gray shirt (never with a tie but always buttoned at the neck and when he was dressed, pinned with a dull gold bar), but his face would be covered, his eyes. Only the shape of his skull would be clear—narrow and long, pointed at the chin, domed at the top—and the color of the skin that covered it, unbroken by a single hair except sparse brows, the color of a penny polished down by years of thumbs till Lincoln's face is a featureless shadow but with red life running beneath. That way he would be resting—not waiting, just resting as if he had worked when all he had done was wake at six and reach to his radio and lie on till seven, hearing music and thinking, then shaving and dressing and spreading his bed and stepping through the yard to the kitchen to eat what my aunt cooked (after she fired the stove if it was winter) —and he would rest till half-past eight when the cook would come and say towards him "Mr. Grant" (they were not good friends) and towards my aunt down the hall, "Miss Ida, here's you a letter," having stopped at the post office on her way. My aunt would come and

stand by the stove and read with lips moving silent and
then say, "Look, Uncle Grant. Here's a letter from
Reynolds." He would look up squinting while she read
out something like, "'Tell Uncle Grant I am thinking
about him this week,'" but before she could read any
more, he would slap his flank and spring to his feet,
rocking in his lacework shoes, opening and shutting his
five-foot-ten like a bellows, and flicking at his
ears—"Great God A-mighty! Where *is* Reynolds?"
When she said "England" he would say, "Over yonder
with them Hitalians and he been thinking about
Grant? Great God A-mighty!" and then trail off into
laughing and then for a long time to come into smiling.
He would be happy that whole day and it is a fact—
there is no one alive or dead I could have made happier with eight or ten words.

But he is dead and the reason I have thought of him
these few days is strange—not because I remembered
some joke on him and certainly not from seeing his
likeness in the blue-black Negroes of the Oxford
streets but because I went in a store to buy postcards
and saw a card from the Berlin Museum—on a black
background an Egyptian head, the tall narrow skull
rocked back on the stalky neck, the chin offered out
like a flickering tongue, the waving lips set in above
(separate as if they were carved by a better man), the
ears with their heavy lobes pinned close to the skull,
and the black-rimmed sockets holding no eyes at all. I
looked on, not knowing why, and turned the card over.
The head was Amenhotep IV, pharaoh of Egypt in the
eighteenth dynasty who canceled the worship of bestial
gods and changed his name to Akhnaton, "it pleases
Aton," the one true god, the streaming disc, the sun. I

bought the card and left the shop and walked ten yards and said to myself in the street what I suddenly knew, "It's the one picture left of Uncle Grant."

HIS FULL NAME AS FAR AS WE KNEW WAS GRANT Terry, and he said he was born near Chatham, Virginia which is some hundred miles to the left of Richmond. (There are still white Terrys near there from whom his family would have taken its name.) He never knew his age but in 1940 when he heard of Old Age Assistance and wanted it (you had to show proof you were sixty-five), my father took him to our doctor who said, "I'll certify him—sure—but if those Welfare Workers took a look at his eyes, they wouldn't need *my* guarantee. He's well past seventy." So assuming he was seventy-five in 1940, that would make him born around 1865— maybe born into freedom and named for a general his parents heard of who set them free—but we didn't know about his youth, what he did to live when he was growing in the years after the war. There was nothing much he could have done but farm for somebody— chopping or picking cotton or ginning cotton or sawing pine timber or at best tending somebody's yard. We did know he had a wife named Ruth who gave him a son named Felix. It is the one thing I recall him telling me from his past (and he told me more than once, never with tears and sometimes with laughing at the end as if it was just his best true story)—"When I left my home in Virginia to come down here, I said to Ruth and my boy, 'I'll see you in Heaven if I don't come back.'" And he never went back.

He came south eighty miles to North Carolina. He told my father he came in a road gang hired by a white contractor to pave the Raleigh streets, but he never said when he came—not to me anyhow, not to anybody still alive. He never said why he came to Macon either. (The streets of Macon are still not paved.) Maybe he had done his Raleigh work and meant to head back to Ruth and Felix but never got farther than sixty miles, stopping in Macon, population two hundred, in Warren County which touches the Virginia line. Or maybe he came to Macon with a railroad gang. (That seems a fair guess. He always called Macon a "seaport town." It was more than a hundred miles from the sea. What he meant was Seaboard Railway—the Norfolk-to-Raleigh tracks split Macon.) Anyhow, he was there by the time I was born in 1933 though he wasn't attached to us, and his work by then —whatever it had been before—was growing things. He planted people's flowers and hoed them, raked dead leaves and burned them, and tended lawns— what lawns there were in Macon where oaktree shade and white sand soil discouraged grass—and then he began tending me.

Not that I needed much tending. My mother was always there and my aunt down the road, and a Negro girl named Millie Mae looked after me in the morning. But sometimes in the evening my parents went visiting or to a picture show (not often, it being the deep Depression), and then Uncle Grant would sit by me while I slept. I don't know why they selected him, *trusted* him, when my aunt could have kept me or Millie Mae. Maybe they thought he could make me grow. (When he first came to Macon and asked for work and somebody said, "What can you do?" he said, "I can make things grow" so they gave him a chance, and he proved it the rest of his life—till my father could say, "Uncle Grant could stick a Coca-Cola bottle in the ground and raise you an ice-cold drink by sunup tomorrow." And God knew I needed growing—I had mysterious convulsions till I was four, sudden blue twitching rigors that rushed me unconscious into sight of death every three or four months.) The best reason though would be that, having no friends of his own, he had taken to me, and there is a joke which seems to show that. One evening when I was nearly two, my parents left me with him, saying they would be back late and that he could sleep in an army cot in my room. But they came back sooner than they expected, and when they drove up under the trees, instead of the house being dark and quiet, there was light streaming from my bedroom and mouth-harp music and laughing enough for a party. In surprise they crept to the porch and peeped in. My high-railed iron bed was by the window, and I was in it in outing pajamas but not lying down—facing Uncle Grant who was standing on the floor playing harp music while I danced in time and laughed. Then he knocked out the spit and passed the harp to me, and I blew what I could while he clapped hands. And then they stopped it—not being angry but saying I had better calm down and maybe Uncle Grant shouldn't pass the harp to me in case of germs (I had already caught gingivitis from chewing a brass doorknob)—and that was our first joke on him.

It went on like that another year—him working the yard off and on and staying with me odd evenings—and then my father changed jobs (*got* a job after six years of failing to sell insurance to wiped-out farmers) and we left Macon, going west a hundred miles to

Asheboro, still in North Carolina, where we lived in a small apartment. Uncle Grant of course stayed on in Macon—he still wasn't ours and we had no lawn of our own, no room for him—but before long my father sent bus fare to my aunt and asked her to put Uncle Grant on the bus (Uncle Grant couldn't read), and soon he arrived for his first visit. He spent the nights in a Negro boardinghouse and the days and evenings in our kitchen. There was nothing he could do to help except wash dishes (he couldn't cook), but help wasn't what my father wanted. He wanted just to talk and every evening after supper, he stayed in the kitchen and talked to Uncle Grant till almost time to sleep. I was too young then to listen—or if I listened, to remember the things they said. They laughed a good deal though—I remember that—and the rest of the time they talked about the past. My mother says they did but *she* didn't listen, and now they are dead and nobody knows why they sat there night after night at a hard kitchen table under a bare light bulb, talking on and on, and laughing. Unless they loved each other—meaning there would come times when they needed to meet, and they never explained the need to themselves. My father would just send bus fare through my aunt or there would be a letter from her saying Uncle Grant was ready for a visit and had asked her to say he was coming, and we would go meet the bus, my father and I—five or six times in the two years we lived in three small rooms.

Then we bought two acres of land in the country near Asheboro and built a house. Or began to. The land needed clearing first—of loblolly pines and blackjack oaks and redbugs and snakes—so Uncle

Grant came and spent the weekdays supervising that. He spent the nights at the same boardinghouse and as far as we knew went nowhere and had no Negro friends, but he spent his Sundays with us. We would pick him up in the car after church—my father and I—and drive out to look at our land. He would tell us what trees had gone that week and beg our pardon for, say, sacrificing a dogwood that had stood in the carpenters' path. But what I remember about those mornings—I was five—are two things he did which changed my mind. One Sunday when the clearing had just begun, the three of us were walking around the land—I in shorts and what I called Jesus-sandals—and as we came to a pile of limbs and weeds, six feet of black snake streamed out. It was May and black snakes go crazy in May so he headed for me and reared on his tail to fight. My father and I were locked stiff in surprise, but before the snake could lash at me, Uncle Grant took one step sideways like lightning and grabbed the snake's tail and cracked him on the air like a leather whip. Then we all breathed deep and looked and laughed at two yards of limp dead snake in Uncle Grant's hand. The way that changed my mind was to make me see Uncle Grant, not as the nurse who sat with me nights or talked on and on to my father, but as a fearless hero to imitate, and I never saw him in the old tame way again, not for eight or nine years. Then another Sunday morning we were walking—the land was clear by this time and building had started, but there wasn't a blade of grass, only mud and thousands of rocks that looked identical to me—and Uncle Grant leaned down quick as he had for the snake and came up with a little rock and handed it to me. It was a perfect Indian arrowhead, and in my joy I said, "How in the world did you see it?" and he said, "I'm three parts Indian myself" which deepened the feeling I had had for him since the snake and also made our two rocky acres something grand—a hunting ground of the Occoneechees or a campsite or even, I hoped, a battlefield (though we never found a second head to prove it).

When the house was finished and we moved in, he came with us. There was one small room off the kitchen where the furnace was, and his bed was there and a little low table to carry the things he owned—in the daytime his shaving equipment and his extra shirt, and at night his precious belongings—an Ingersoll watch and a pocketknife. In the daytime he worked to grow us a lawn, and gradually, single-handed, he grew us a beauty. And once it was strong, he began to cut it—with a small hand sickle and his pocketknife. We had a lawn mower and he tried to use it but stopped, saying rocks were too plentiful still—the real reason being he could cut grass better, cut it *right*, by hand and if that meant bending to the ground all day at age about seventy-five and trimming two acres with a three-inch blade, then that was all right. It was what he could do, in spring and summer. In the fall he raked leaves, not waiting till the trees were bare and taking them all at once but raking all day every day. It was one of our jokes on him (a true joke—they were all true) that we once saw him run a few yards and catch a dead leaf as it fell, in the air, and grind it to dust in his hand. In the evening after us he ate at the kitchen counter and washed all our dishes and then went into his room and sat on his bed and looked at picture magazines. Sometimes my father would sit with him and I would fly in and out, but most of the time he sat in silence, thinking whatever his private thoughts were, till we gave him a radio.

That was Christmas 1939 and there wasn't much to hear except black war news, but nothing we gave him ever pleased him more. Not that he had seemed unhappy before—I don't think he thought about happiness—but now he would sit there on into the night. I would sit beside him long as my mother allowed in the dark (the only light was the radio dial), hearing our favorite things which were short-wave programs in German and Spanish with Morse Code bursting in like machine-gun fire to make us laugh. We didn't understand a word and my father who thought we were fools would step to the door and shake his head at us in the dark, but Uncle Grant would slap his thigh and say, "*Listen* to them Hitalians, Mr. Will!" *Hitalians* was what he called all foreigners, and "Great God A-mighty" was his favorite excited expression, the one he used every time some Spaniard would speed up the news or "The Star-Spangled Banner" would play so before long of course I was saying it too—age six. At first I just said it with him when he laughed, but once I slipped and said it in front of my mother, and she asked him not to curse around me and made me stay out of his room for a while. With me being punished my father filled the gap by spending more time in the furnace room, and it was then the jokes piled up. Despite all the war news, he would have a new joke every evening—my father, that is, on Uncle Grant. One night for instance after they had sat an hour listening, they switched off the radio to let it cool and to talk.

They talked quite awhile till my father said, "Let's switch it on. It's time for the midnight news" so they did, and there was the news, waiting for them. When it had finished and music had begun, Uncle Grant said, "When does they sleep, Mr. Will?" My father said "Who?" and he said—pointing through the dark to the radio—"Them little peoples in yonder." My father whose work was electrical supplies explained about waves in the air without wires and Uncle Grant nodded. But some time later when they had sat up extra-late, Uncle Grant asked if it wasn't bedtime. My father took the hint but was slow about leaving—standing in the door, hearing the end of some program—so Uncle Grant stood and unbuttoned his collar, then thought and switched off the radio. My father said, "How come you did that?" and he said, "I can't undress with them little peoples watching, Mr. Will." So my father never tried explaining again.

Then after three years we lost the house and all that grass and had to move to another apartment in Asheboro. By then I had a year-old brother named Bill so again there was no room for Uncle Grant and nothing for him to do if there had been, and my father explained it a month in advance—that much as we wanted him around, we couldn't keep paying him three dollars a week just to wash dishes and that if he stayed on in Asheboro he would have to find someplace to sleep and hire-out to other people to pay his rent. He told my father he would think it over, and he thought that whole last month, asking no advice, sitting by himself most evenings as I was in school and busy and my father was ashamed in his presence, and giving no sign of his plans till the day we moved. He helped that day by packing china and watching how the movers treated our furniture, and when everything had gone except his few belongings, my father said, "Where are you going, Uncle Grant?" He said, "I'm sleeping in that boardinghouse till I get you all's windows washed. Then I'm going to Macon on the bus. I ain't hiring-out in this town." (Asheboro was a stocking-mill town.) My father said, "You might break your radio on the bus. Wait till Sunday and I'll carry you." Uncle Grant said, "I been studying that—where am I going to plug in a radio in Macon? You keep it here and if I wants it I'll let you know." My father said, "Maybe when I get a little money I can trade it in on a battery set," and he said "Maybe you can" and two days later went to Macon by bus, saying he would stay with a Negro named Rommie Watson till he found a house. But somewhere in the hundred miles, for some reason, he changed his mind and when the bus set him down, he walked to my aunt's back door and asked could he sleep in her old smokehouse till he found a place of his own? She knew of course why we turned him loose so she told him Yes, and he swept it out and slept on an army cot, coming to her kitchen for meals but not eating well, not looking for a house of his own, not saying a word about work. My aunt finally asked him was he all right, and he said, "I will be soon as I get my bearings." In about two weeks he came in to breakfast with the cot rolled under his arm and his bag of belongings. When he had eaten he said he had found a house at the far end of Macon—a one-room house under oak trees in the yard of a Negro church. Then he left and was gone all day, all night, but my aunt looked out in the morning and there he was, trimming her bushes, having got some sort of bearings, enough to last two years.

We had turned him loose in 1942. He lived on thirteen years and he never let us take hold again. We stayed in Asheboro three years after he left—two years in that apartment and a year in a good-sized house—but he didn't come to visit in all that time. I don't know whether we asked him and if we did, what reason he gave for refusing. He just didn't come and he might have said he was too old. But he worked for my aunt every day, strong as ever, still trimming what he grew with a pocketknife, and the only way he showed age was by not taking supper in my aunt's kitchen. In summer he would stop about six, in winter about five—before dark—and put up his tools and come to the back door, and my aunt would give him cold biscuits and sometimes a little jar of syrup or preserves, and he would walk home a mile and a half and spend his evenings by a kerosene lamp, alone. But that was no change for him, being by himself.

What *was* a change was that after he had been back in Macon two years, he fell in some sort of love with a girl named Katie. She was not from Macon but had come there as cook to a cousin of ours who returned so she had no Negro friends either, and though she was no more than twenty, she began to sit with him some evenings. My aunt didn't know if they got beyond sitting, but she didn't worry much, not at first. Uncle Grant was pushing eighty and it seemed at first that Katie was good to him in ways that made him happy. My aunt *did* say to him once, "Uncle Grant, don't let that girl take your money away," and he said, "No'm. Every penny I lends her, she pay me back." But then it

turned bad. After six months or so Katie began taking
him to Warrenton on Saturdays (the county seat, five
miles away), and they would drink fifty-cent wine
called "Sneaky Pete," and every week he would have
the few hairs shaved off his head (to hide them from
Katie as they were white). For a while he managed to
keep his drinking to Saturdays and to be cold-sober
when he turned up for Sunday breakfast so my aunt
didn't complain but finally he slipped. One Sunday he
came in late—about nine—walking straight and of
course dressed clean but old around the eyes and with
his hat still on. He said "Good morning" and sat by the
green kitchen table. My aunt said the same and, not
really noticing, gave him a dish of cornflakes. He ate a
few spoonfuls in silence. Then he sprang to the floor
and slapped his flank and said, "What is the meaning
of *this*?"—so loud she could smell the wine and pointing at his bowl. My aunt went over and there was a
needle in his food. Thinking fast, she laughed and said,
"Excuse me, Uncle Grant. I was sewing in here this
week and somebody came to the door, and I stuck the
needle in the cereal box, and it must have worked
through." That was the truth and, sober, he would
have known it, but he stood there rocking a little and
then said, "Somebody trying to kill me is all *I* know."
My aunt said, "If you are that big a fool, you can leave
my house" so he stood another minute and then he
left.

That was in late October—he had just started raking leaves. His shame kept him home the following
day—and for two months to come. My aunt reckoned
he would come back when he got hungry but he didn't.
What food he got he bought from his neighbors or

maybe Katie sneaked him things from our cousin's kitchen, but he didn't show up at my aunt's, and every leaf fell and thousands of acorns, and she finally hired boys to clear them. He still hadn't showed up by Christmas when we arrived for three days. That was the first we knew of his shame. My father said, "To be sure, he'll show up to see me," but my aunt said, "You are the *last* one he wants to see, feeling like he does," and my father saw she was right. We had brought him a box of Brown Mule chewing tobacco. He surely knew that—we gave him that every Christmas—and we waited but he didn't come. When we left on the 27th my father gave my aunt the Brown Mule and told her to save it till Uncle Grant showed up. She said in that case it would be bone-dry by the time he got it.

But for once she was wrong. About two weeks later in a hard cold spell his house burned down in the night from an overheated stove. My aunt heard that from her cook in the morning and heard that he got out unharmed with the clothes on his back so she packed a lard bucket with food and set our tobacco on top and sent it by the cook to where he was, which was at some neighbor's. The cook came back and said he thanked her and that afternoon he came. My aunt was nodding but the cook waked her and said, "Mr. Grant's out yonder on the porch, Miss Ida." She went and told him she was sorry to hear of his trouble and what was he going to do now? He said, "I don't hardly know but could I just sleep in the smokehouse till I get my bearings?" She thought and said, "Yes, if you'll stay there without having company." He knew who she meant and nodded and spent the rest of the day cleaning the smokehouse and getting the woodstove fit to use.

He stayed there without having company, working on the yard by day and on the smokehouse by night. It was just one room, twice as tall as wide, with pine walls and floor. He scrubbed every board—cold as it was—and when they were dry, tacked newspapers around the walls high as he could reach to keep out wind. And as winter passed he kept finding things to do to that one room till it looked as if he took it to be his home. So when spring came my aunt hired a carpenter, and he put plasterboard on the walls and linoleum underfoot and a lock on the door. Then she took back the army cot and bought an old iron bed and a good felt mattress and gave Uncle Grant a key to the door, saying, "This is your key. I'll keep the spare one in case you lose it." But he never lost it and he lived on there, having got the bearings, somehow or other, that lasted the rest of his life.

We moved back to Warren County in 1945. My father got a job that let him live in Warrenton (or travel from there, selling freezers to farmers), and we lived in a hotel apartment, still with no yard of our own. But Sunday afternoons we would drive the five miles to Macon for supper with my aunt. When we got there we would sit an hour and talk, and then my father would rise and say he was stepping out back to see Uncle Grant and who wanted to come? That was a signal for me to say "Me," and for a year or so I said it and followed him to the smokehouse. Uncle Grant would have been waiting all afternoon and talk would begin by him asking me about school and what I was doing. I was twelve and wasn't doing much but keeping a diary so my answers wouldn't take long, and he would turn to my father, and they would begin where they left off the week before in the circles of remembering and laughing. Old as I was, I still didn't listen, but soon as they got underway, I would stand and walk round the room, reading the papers on the walls till I knew them by heart. (What I *did* hear was, week after week, my father offering to take Uncle Grant on one of his Virginia business trips and detour to Chatham so he could look up Felix his son and Ruth his wife if she was alive. Uncle Grant would say, "That's a good idea. Let me know when you fixing to go." But he never went. He rode with my father a number of times— down into South Carolina and as far west as Charlotte —but whenever they set the date for a trip to Virginia and the date drew near, Uncle Grant would find yard work that couldn't wait or get sick a day or two with rheumatism.) But a year of such Sundays passed, and I slowed down on the smokehouse visits. My father would rise as before and ask who was going with him to Uncle Grant's, and more and more my brother volunteered, not me. He was going on six, the age I had been when Uncle Grant cracked the snake and found me the arrowhead and we listened to Hitalian news together, so he stepped into whatever place Uncle Grant kept for me and gradually filled more and more of it. But not all, never all, because every time my father came back from a visit he would say, "Uncle Grant asked after you. Step out yonder and speak to him, son." I would look up from what I was doing— seventh-grade arithmetic or a Hardy Boys mystery— and say, "Soon as I finish this," and of course before I finished, it would be dark and supper would be ready. But I always saw him after supper when he came in to eat and to wash our dishes—little fidgety meetings with nothing to talk about but how he was feeling and with gaps of silence getting longer and longer till I would say "Goodbye" and he would say "All right" and I would hurry out. (Occasionally though, he would move some way that detained me—by dropping the dishrag, say, and old as he was, stooping for it in a flash that recalled him reaching bare-handed for the snake to save me—and I would find things to say or look on awhile at his slow body, seeing how grand he had been and knowing how happy I could make him, just waiting around.)

It went on like that till the summer of 1947. Then we moved again—sixty miles, to Raleigh, into a house with two good yards and a steam-heated basement room—and as my father arranged, Uncle Grant followed in a day or so. He had not volunteered to follow, even when my father described the basement room and the grass and privet hedge that, since it was August were nearly out of hand, so my father asked him—"Would you come up and help us get straight?" and he said, "I'll ask Miss Ida can I take off a week." She gave him the week and we gave him the fare and he came. He started next morning at the ankle-high grass, and by sundown he had cut a patch about twenty feet square and sat in the kitchen, bolt-upright but too tired to eat. My father saw the trouble and saw a way out—he said, "I am driving to Clinton tomorrow. Come on and keep me company in this heat." Uncle Grant accepted, not mentioning grass. And none of us mentioned it again. When they got back from Clinton two evenings later, he spent one night, and the next day he went to Macon for good. Busy as my father was, he took Uncle Grant by car and spent a night at my aunt's. Then he came back to Raleigh and at supper that evening said, "He is older than I counted on him being. He won't last long. So I bought him a battery radio to keep him company."

He was maybe eight-two when he tackled our new lawn and lost. My father was forty-seven. Uncle Grant lasted eight years, working on my aunt's yard till eight months before he died (no slower than ever and with nothing but a boy to rake up behind him), spending his evenings with nothing but his battery radio (Katie having drunk herself jobless and vanished), complaining of nothing but sometimes numb feet, asking for nothing but Brown Mule tobacco (and getting that whenever we visited, especially at Christmas). My father lasted six.

He died in February, 1954—my father. Cancer of the lung with tumors the size of bird eggs clustered in his throat which nobody noticed till he thought he had bronchitis and called on a doctor. It went very quickly —twenty-one days—and my aunt didn't tell Uncle Grant till she had to. Hoping for the best, she had seen no reason to upset him in advance, but when we phoned her that Sunday night, she put on her coat and went to the smokehouse and knocked. Uncle Grant cracked the door and seeing it was her (she had never called on him after dark before), said, "What's wrong, Miss Ida?" She stood on the doorstep—half of a granite millstone—and said, "Will Price is dead." The heat of his room rushed past her into the dark, and directly he said, "Sit down, Miss Ida," pointing behind him to his single chair. She was my *mother's* sister but she stepped in and sat on his chair, and he sat on the edge of his mattress. Some radio music played on between them, and according to her, he never asked a question but waited. So when she got breath enough, she said the funeral was Tuesday and that he could ride down with her and her son if he wanted to. He thought and said, "Thank you, no'm. I better set here," and she went home to bed. In the morning after his breakfast, he stepped to her bedroom door and called her out and handed her three dollar bills to go towards flowers and she took them. He didn't work all that day or come in again for food so she sent his supper by the cook who reported he wasn't sick, but before she left Tuesday morning for Raleigh, he was stripping ivy off the lightninged oak, too busy to do more than wave goodbye as the car rolled down to the road.

He just never mentioned my father, that was all— for his own reasons, never spoke my father's name in anybody's hearing again. My aunt came back from the funeral and gave him a full description, and he said, "It sounds mighty nice," and ever after that if she brought up the subject—remembering some joke of my father's for instance—he would listen and laugh a little if that was expected but at the first break, get up and leave the room. He went on speaking of others who were someway gone—Ruth his wife and Felix his son and once or twice even Katie—but never my father, not even the last time I saw him.

That was Christmas of 1954 and by then he was flat on his back in a Welfare Home near Warrenton, had been there nearly four months. Six months after my father's death, his feet and legs went back on him totally. He couldn't stand for more than ten minutes without going numb from his waist down, and one night he fell, going to the smokehouse from supper—

on his soft grass—so he took his bed, and when he didn't come to breakfast, my aunt went out and hearing of the fall, asked her doctor to come. He came and privately told her nothing was broken—it was poor circulation which would never improve, and didn't she want him to find Uncle Grant a place with nurses? There was nothing she could do but agree, being old herself, and the doctor found space in the house of a woman named Sarah Cawthon who tended old Negroes for the Welfare Department. Then my aunt asked Uncle Grant if going there wasn't the wise thing for him—where he could rest with attention and regular meals and plenty of company and his radio and where she could visit him Saturdays, headed for Warrenton? He thought and said "Yes'm, it is," and she bought him two suits of pajamas and a flannel robe (he had always slept in long underwear), and they committed him early in September—her and her son—as the end of summer slammed down.

We didn't visit Macon in a body that Christmas. My mother wasn't up to it so we spent the day in Raleigh, but early on the 26th I drove to Macon to deliver our gifts and collect what was waiting for us. I stayed with my aunt most of the day, and her children and grandchildren came in for dinner, but after the eating, things got quiet and people took pains not to speak of the past, and at four o'clock I loaded up and said goodbye. My aunt followed me to the car and kissed me and said, "Aren't you going to stop by Sarah Cawthon's and see Uncle Grant?" I looked at the sky to show it was late, and she said, "It won't take long and nobody God made will appreciate it more." So I stopped by and knocked on the holly-wreathed door

and Sarah Cawthon came. I said I would like to see
Grant Terry, and she said, "Yes sir. Who is calling?" I
smiled at that and said "Reynolds Price." —"Mr. Will
Price's boy?" —"His oldest boy." She smiled too and
said he was waiting for me and headed for a back bedroom. I paused at the door and she went ahead, flicking on the light, saying, "Mr. Grant, here's you a
surprise." Then she walked out and I walked in, and
the first thing I noticed was his neck. He was sitting up
in bed in his clean pajamas. They were buttoned to the
top, but they had no collar and his neck was bare. That
was the surprise. I had just never seen it before, not
down to his shoulders, and the sight of it now—so lean
and long but the skin drawn tight—surprised me. *He*
was not surprised. He had known *some* Price would
turn up at Christmas, and seeing it was me, he
laughed, "Great God A-mighty, Reynolds, you bigger
than me." (I was twenty-one. I had reached my full
growth some time before, but he still didn't say "*Mr.*
Reynolds.") Then he pointed to a corner of the room
where a two-foot plastic Christmas tree stood on a
table, hung with a paper chain but no lights. There
were two things under the tree on tissue paper—some
bedroom shoes from my aunt and the box of Brown
Mule my mother had mailed without telling me—and
he said, "I thank you for my present," meaning the
tobacco which he had not opened. I noticed when he
laughed that his teeth were gone and remembered my
aunt commenting on the strangeness of that—how his
teeth had vanished since he took his bed, just dissolved
with nobody's help. So the Brown Mule was useless,
like the shoes. He never stood up anymore, he said.
But that was the nearest he came to speaking of his

health, and I didn't ask questions except to say did he have a radio? He said "Two" and pointed to his own battery set on the far side of him and across the room to one by an empty bed. I asked whose that was and he said, "Freddy's. The Nigger that sleeps yonder." I asked where was Freddy now and he said, "Spending some time with his family, thank God. All that ails him is his water." But before he explained Freddy's symptoms, Sarah Cawthon returned with orange juice for both of us and a slice of fruitcake for me. Then she smoothed the sheets around Uncle Grant and said to him, "Tell Mr. Reynolds your New Year's resolution." He said, "What you driving at?" So she told me—"Mr. Grant's getting baptized for New Year. He's been about to run me crazy to get him baptized—ain't you, Mr. Grant?" He didn't answer, didn't look at her or me but down at his hands on the sheet, and she went on—"Yes sir, he been running me *crazy* to get him baptized, old as he is, so I have arranged it for New Year's Day with my preacher. I got a big old trough in the back yard, and we are bringing that in the kitchen and spreading a clean sheet in it and filling it up with nice warm water, and *under* he's going—ain't you Mr. Grant?" Still looking down, he said he would think it over. She said, "Well, of course you are and we wish Mr. Reynolds could be here to see it, don't we?" Then she took our glasses and left. When her steps had faded completely, he looked up at me and said, "I ain't going to be baptized in no hog trough." I said I was sure it wasn't a hog trough, but if he didn't want to be dipped, I saw no reason why he should. He said, "It ain't *me* that wants it. It's that woman. She come in here—last week, I believe—and asked me was I baptized and I said, 'No, not to my knowledge' so she said, 'Don't you know you can't get to Heaven and see your folks till you baptized?'" He waited a moment and asked me, "Is that the truth?" And straight off I said, "No. You'll see everybody you want to see, I'm sure. Give them best wishes from me!" He laughed, "I'll do that thing," then was quiet a moment, and not looking at me, said, "There *is* two or three I hope to meet, but I ain't studying the rest." Then he looked and said, "You're sure about that?—what you just now told me?" and again not waiting I said I was sure so he smiled, and I reckoned I could leave. I stepped to his window and looked out at what was almost night—"Uncle Grant, I better be heading home." He said "Thank you, sir" (not saying what for), and I stopped at the foot of his bed and asked what I had to ask, what my father would have asked—"Is there any little thing I can do for you?" He said "Not a thing." I said, "You are not still worried about being baptized, are you?" and he said, "No, you have eased my mind. I can tell that woman *my* mind is easy, and if she want to worry, that's *her* red wagon." I laid my hand on the ridge of sheet that was his right foot—"If you need anything, tell Aunt Ida, and she'll either get it or let us know." He said, "I won't need nothing." Then I stepped to the door and told him "Goodbye," and he said "Thank you" again (still not saying what for) and —grinning—that he would see me in Heaven if not any sooner. I grinned too and walked easy down Sarah Cawthon's hall and made it to the door without being heard and got in the car and started the sixty miles to Raleigh in full night alone, wondering part of the way (maybe fifteen minutes), "Have I sent him to Hell with my theology?" but knowing that was just a joke and smiling to myself and driving on, thinking gradually of my own business, not thinking of him at all, not working back to what he had been in previous days, feeling I had no reasons.

AND WENT ON TILL LATE LAST WEEK—NEARLY SEVEN years—not thinking of him more than, say fifteen seconds at a stretch, not even when he died just before his afternoon nap, the May after I saw him in December. Freddy his roommate told my aunt, "I was making another police dog and he died"—Freddy made dogs to sell, out of socks and knitting wool—and she and her son handled the funeral. We didn't go, my part of the family (my mother had a job by then and I was deep in college exams and my brother was too young to drive), but my mother sent flowers and they buried him at Mount Zion Church which he never attended, a mile from my aunt's, not in a Welfare coffin but in one she paid for, in a grave I have never seen.

Yet because of an accident—stopping to buy postcards—I have spent a week, three thousand miles from home, thinking of nothing but him, working back to what he may have been, to what we knew anyhow, finding I knew a good deal, finding *reasons*, and thinking how happy he would be if he could know, how long he would laugh, rocking in his lacework shoes, if he heard what reminded me of him (a Hitalian face on a card—Amenhotep IV, pharaoh of Egypt in the eighteenth dynasty who fathered six daughters but no son on Nefertiti his queen and canceled the worship of hawks and bulls and changed his name to Akhnaton, "it pleases Aton," the single god, the sun that causes growth)—and him the son of Negro slaves, named Grant maybe for the Union general (a name he could not recognize or write), who grew up near Chatham, Virginia, and made his one son Felix on a woman named Ruth and left them both to go south to work and somehow settled in Macon near us, finally with us (claiming he could make things grow, which he could), and tended me nights when I was a baby and our yard when we had one and for his own reasons loved my father and was loved by him and maybe loved me, *trusted* me enough to put his salvation in my hands that last day I saw him (him about ninety and me twenty-one) and believed what I said—that in Heaven he would meet the few folks he missed—and claimed he would see me there. And this is the point, this is what I know after this last week—that final joke, if it *was* a joke (him saying he would see me in Heaven), who-ever it was on, it was not on him.

THE NAMES AND
FACES OF HEROES

AFTER AN HOUR I BELIEVE IT AND THINK, "WE are people in love. We flee through hard winter night. What our enemies want is to separate us. Will we end together? Will we end alive?" And my lips part to ask him, but seeing his face in dashboard light (his gray eyes set on the road and the dark), I muffle my question and know the reason— "We have not broke silence for an hour by the clock. We must flee on silent. Maybe if we speak even close as we are, we will speak separate tongues after so long a time." I shut my eyes, press hard with the lids till my mind's eye opens, then balloon it light through roof through steel, set it high and cold in January night, staring down to see us whole. First we are one black car on a slim strip of road laid white through pines,

drawn slowly west by the hoop of light we cast ahead
—the one light burning for fifty miles, it being past
eleven, all farms and houses crouched into sleep, all
riders but us. Then my eye falls downward, hovers on
the roof in the wind we make, pierces steel, sees us
close—huddled on the worn mohair of a 1939 Pontiac,
he slumped huge at the wheel, I the thin fork of flesh
thrust out of his groin on the seat beside him, my dark
head the burden in his lap his only hollow that flushes
beneath me with rhythm I predict to force blood
against my weight through nodes of tissue, squabs of
muscle that made me ten years ago, made half anyhow,
he being my father and I being nine, we heading towards home not fleeing, silent as I say, my real eyes
shut, his eyes on nothing but road. So we are not
lovers nor spies nor thieves and speaking for me, my
foes are inward not there in the night. My mind's eye
enters me calm again, and I brace to look, to say
"How much further?" but he drops a hand which stalls
me, testing my flannel pajamas for warmth, ringing my
ankle and shin and ticklish knee (in earnest, tight not
gentle), slipping between two buttons of the coat to
brush one breast then out again and down to rest on
my hip. His thumb and fingers ride the high saddle
bone, the fat of his hand in the hollow *I* have, heavy
but still on the dry knots of boyish equipment waiting
for life to start. I roll back on my head to see him
again, to meet his eyes. He looks on forward so I go
blind again and slide my right hand to his, probing
with a finger till I find his only wound—a round yellow socket beneath his thumb where he shot himself
when he was eight, by surprise, showing off his father's
pistol to friends (the one fool thing I know he has

done). My finger rests there and we last that way maybe two or three miles while the road is straight. Then a curve begins. He says "Excuse me, Preacher" in his natural voice and takes his hand. My eyes stay blind and I think what I know, "I love you tonight more than all my life before"—think it in *my* natural voice. But I do not say it, and I do not say I excuse him though I do. I open my eyes on his face in dashboard light.

I search it for a hero. For the first time. I have searched nearly every other face since last July, the final Sunday at camp when a minister told us, "The short cut to being a man is finding your hero, somebody who is what you are not but need to be. What I mean is this. Examine yourself. When you find what your main lack is, seek that in some great man. Say your trouble is fear—you are scared of the dark, scared of that bully in your grade at school, scared of striking out when you come up to bat. Take some great brave, some warrior—Douglas MacArthur, Enos Slaughter. Say your trouble is worse. Say it's telling lies. Take George Washington—personal heroes don't need to be living just so they lived once. Read a book about him. Study his picture. (You may think he looks a little stiff. That is because his teeth were carved out of cypress. A man makes his face and making a good one is as hard a job as laying road through solid rock, and Washington made himself as fine a face as any man since Jesus—and He was not a man.) Then imitate him. Chin yourself on his example and you will be a man before you need a razor." I need to be a man hard as anybody so riding home from camp and that sermon, I sat among lanyards I plaited and whistles I

carved and searched my life for the one great lack my
foe. He had mentioned lacking courage—that minister. I lack it. I will not try to do what I think I cannot
do well such as make friends or play games where
somebody hands you a ball and bat and asks the world
of you, asks you to launch without thinking some act
on the air with natural grace easy as laughing. He had
mentioned lying. I lie every day—telling my mother
for instance that the weeks at camp were happy when
what I did was by day whittle all that trashy equipment, climb through snakes in July sun with brogans
grating my heels, swim in ice water with boys that
would just as soon drown you as smile and by night
pray for three large things—that I not wet the bed,
that I choke the homesickness one more day, that
these five weeks vanish and leave no sign no memory.
But they were only two on a string of lacks which
unreeled behind me that Sunday riding home from
camp (unseen beyond glass the hateful tan rock turning to round pine hills where Randolph is and home),
and on the string were selfishness to Marcia my cousin
who is my main friend and gives me whatever she has,
envy of my brother who is one year old and whose
arms I purposely threw out of joint three months ago,
envy of people my age who do so easily things I will
not and thus lock together in tangles of friendship,
pride in the things I can do which they cannot (but half
pride at worst as the things I can do, they do not want
to do—drawing, carving, solo singing. I am Randolph's leading boy soprano and was ashamed to be till
a Saturday night last August when I sang to a room of
sweating soldiers at the U.S.O. I was asked by the
hostess for something patriotic, but I thought they

would not need that on their weekend off any more than they needed me in Buster Brown collar and white short pants so I sang Brahms' *Lullaby* which you can hum if you forget, and if it was a mistake, they never let on. I do not mean anybody cried. They kept on swallowing Coca-Colas and their boots kept smelling, but they shut up talking and clapped at the end, and as I left the platform and aimed for the door blistered with shame, one lone soldier gave me the blue and gold enamel shield off his cap, saying "Here you are"), and far graver things—wishing death nightly on two boys I know, breaking God's law about honoring parents by failing to do simple things they ask such as look at people when I talk, by doubting they can care for me daily (when my mother thinks of little else and Father would no more sleep without kissing me goodnight than he would strike me), sometimes doubting I am theirs at all but just some orphan they took in kindness. I made that list without trying seven months ago, and it has grown since then. Whenever I speak or move these days new faults stare out of my heart. The trouble though is I still do not know my greatest lack, my *mortal* foe. Any one if I stare back long enough seems bound to sink me. So I seek a hero grand enough to take on all my lacks, but for seven months now I have looked—looked hard—and am nowhere near him. Who *is* there these days, who has there ever been broad enough, grand enough to stand day and night and ward off all my foes? Nobody, I begin to think. I have looked everywhere I know to look, first in books I had or bought for the purpose—*Little People Who Became Great* (Abraham Lincoln, Helen Keller, Andrew Carnegie), *Minute Lives of Great Men and Women* (a page and a picture for everybody including Stephen Foster), and a set called *Living Biographies of Great Composers, Philosophers, Prophets, Poets and Statesmen*. I have not read books that do not show faces because I study a man's face first. Then if that calls me on, I read his deeds. I read for three months and taking deeds and faces together, I settled on Caesar Augustus and Alexander the Great as final candidates. They were already great when they were young, and they both wore faces like hard silver medals awarded for lasting—I got that much from *Minute Lives*—so I thought they were safe and that I would read further and then choose one. But as I read they fell in before me—Alexander crushing that boy's head who brought bad news and when they were lost in a desert and famished and his men found one drink of water and gladly brought it to him in a helmet, him pouring it out in the sand to waste, and Augustus leading the wives of his friends into private rooms during public banquets, making them do what they could not refuse. All the dead have failed me. That is why I study my father tonight. He is the last living man I know or can think of that I have not considered, which is no slight to him—you do not seek heroes at home. No, when the dead played out, I turned to my autographs and started there. I have written to famous men for over a year since the war began. I write on Boy Scout stationery (I am not a Scout), give my age and ask for their names in ink. I have got answers from several generals on the battlefield (MacArthur who sent good luck from the Philippines, Mark Clark who typed a note from secret headquarters, Eisenhower who said in his wide leaning hand, "I do not think it would be possible for me to refuse a nine-year-old American anything I could do for him"), from most of Roosevelt's cabinet (but not from him though I have three notes from Miss Grace Tully to say he does not have time and neither does his wife), from Toscanini and a picture of Johnny Weissmuller on a limb crouched with his bare knife to leap, saying "Hello from Tarzan your friend." But studying them I saw I could not know enough to decide. They are surely famous but I cannot see them or watch them move, and until they die and their secrets appear, how can I know they are genuine heroes?—that they do not have yawning holes of their own which they hide? So from them I have turned to men I can watch and hear, and since I seldom travel this means the men I am kin to. I will not think against my blood, but of all my uncles and cousins (my grandfathers died before I was born), the two I love and that seem to love me—that listen when I speak—and that have dark happy faces are the ones who are liable at any time to start drinking and disappear spending money hand over fist in Richmond or Washington until they are broke and wire for my father who drives up and finds them in a bar with a new suit on and a rosebud and some temporary friends and brings them home to their wives. My father has one brother who fought in France in the First World War and was playing cards in a hole one night when a bomb landed, and when he came to, he picked up his best friend who was quiet at his side and crawled with him half a mile before he saw that the friend lacked a head, but later he was gassed and retired from battle so that now, sitting or standing, he slumps round a hole in his chest and scrapes up blood every hour or two even summer nights visiting on our porch from Tennessee his home. My other male kin live even farther away or do not notice me or are fat which is why as I say I have come to my father tonight—my head rolled back on his lap, my ears sunk in his shifting kernels so I cannot hear only see, my eyes strained up through his arms to his face.

It is round as a watch when he does not smile which he does not now, and even in warm yellow light of speedometer-amp-meter-oil pressure gauges, it is red as if he was cold, as if there was no plate glass to hold off the wind we make rushing home. It is always red and reddest I know, though I cannot see, under his collar on the back of his neck where the hair leaves off. There is not much hair anywhere on his head. It has vanished two inches back on his forehead, and where it starts it is dark but seems no color or the color of shadows in old photographs. Above his ears it is already white (he is forty-two and the white is real, but five years ago when it was not, I was singing in bed one night "When I Grow Too Old To Dream," and he heard me and went to the toilet and powdered his hair and came and stood in the door ghostly, old with the hall light behind him and said, "I am too old to dream, Preacher." I sang on a minute, looking, and then cried "Stop. Stop," and wept which of course he did not intend), and each morning he wets it and brushes every strand at least five minutes till it lies on his skull like paint and stays all day. It is one of his things you cannot touch. His glasses are another. He treats them kindly as if they were delicate people—unrimmed octagons hooked to gold wires that ride the start of his firm long nose and loop back over his large flat ears—

and in return they do not hide his eyes which are gray
and wide and which even in the dark draw light to
them so he generally seems to be thinking of fun when
he may be thinking we have lost our house (we have
just done that) or his heart is failing (he thinks his
heart stood still last Christmas when he was on a lad-
der swapping lights in our tree, and whenever I look
he is taking his pulse). And with all his worries it
mostly *is* fun he thinks because when he opens his
mouth, if people are there they generally laugh—with
him or at him, he does not mind which. I know a string
of his jokes as long as the string of my personal lacks,
and he adds on new ones most days he feels well
enough. A lot of his jokes of course I do not understand but I no longer ask. I used to ask and he would
say, "Wait a little, Preacher. Your day will come" so I
hold them mysterious in my skull till the day they burst
into meaning. But most of his fun is open to view, to
anybody's eyes that will look because what he mainly
loves is turning himself into other people before your
eyes. Whenever in the evenings we visit our friends,
everybody will talk awhile including my father, and
then he may go silent and stare into space, pecking his
teeth with a fingernail till his eyes come back from
where they have been and his long lips stretch straight
which is how he smiles, and then whoever we are visiting—if he has been watching my father—will know to
say, "Mock somebody for us, Jeff." ("Mocking" is
what most people call it. My father calls it "taking people off.") He will look sheepish a minute, then lean
forward in his chair—and I sitting on the rug, my
heart will rise for I know he has something to give us
now—and looking at the floor say, "Remember how

Dr. Tucker pulled teeth?" Everybody will grin Yes but somebody (sometimes me) will say "How?" and he will start becoming Dr. Tucker, not lying, just seriously turning himself into that old dentist—greeting his patient at the door, bowing him over to the chair (this is when he shrinks eight inches, dries, goes balder still, hikes his voice up half a scale), talking every step to soothe the patient, sneaking behind him, rinsing his rusty pullers at the tap, cooing "Open your mouth, sweet *thing*," leaping on the mouth like a boa constrictor, holding up the tooth victorious, smiling "*There* he is and you didn't even feel it, did you, darling?" Then he will be Jeff McCraw again, hitching up his trousers with the sides of his wrists, leading us into the laughter. When it starts to die somebody will say, "Jeff, you beat all. You missed your calling. You ought to be in the movies," and if he is not worried that night he may move on through one or two more transformations— Miss Georgie Ballard singing in church with her head like an owl swivelling, Mrs. V. L. Womble on her velvet pillow, President Roosevelt in a "My friends" speech, or on request little pieces of people—Mr. Jim Bender's walk, Miss Amma Godwin's hand on her stomach. But it suits me more when he stops after one. That way I can laugh and take pride in his gifts, but if he continues I may take fright at him spinning on through crowds of old people, dead people, people I do not know as if his own life—his life with us—is not enough. One such night when he was happy and everybody was egging him on I cried to him "Stop" before it was too late and ran from the room. I am not known as a problem so people notice when I cry. My mother came behind me at once and sitting in a cold stairwell, calmed me while I made up a reason for what I had done. She said, "Let your father have a little fun. He does not have much." I remembered how often she warned me against crossing my eyes at school to make children laugh, saying they might get stuck, so I told her he might stick and then we would carry him home as Dr. Tucker or Mrs. Womble or Miss Lula Fleming at the Baptist organ. That was a lie but it was all I knew, all I could offer on such short notice to justify terror, and telling it made us laugh, calmed me, stopped me thinking of reasons. And I did not worry or think of my terror again till several months later when he came in disguise. It was not the first time he had worn disguise (half the stories about him are about his disguises), but he did not wear it often, and though I was seven I had never seen him that way before. Maybe it is why he came that night, thinking I was old enough and would like the joke since I loved his other fun. Anyhow the joke was not for me but for Uncle Hawk, an old colored man who lived with us. I was just the one who answered the door. It was night of course. I had finished my supper and leaving the others, had gone to the living room and was on the floor by the radio. After a while there came a knock on the panes of the door. I said, "I will get it" to the empty room, thinking they were all in the kitchen, turned on the porch light and opened the door on a tall man heavy-set with white hair, a black derby hat, a black overcoat to his ankles, gray kid gloves, a briefcase, a long white face coiled back under pinch-nose glasses looking down. It was nobody I knew, nobody I had seen and what could he sell at this time of night? My heart seized like a fist and I thought, "He has come for me" (as I say, it is my darkest fear that I am not the blood child of Jeff and Rhew McCraw, that I was adopted at birth, that someday a strange man will come and rightfully claim me). But still looking down he said, "Does an old colored man named Hawk work here?" and I tore to the kitchen for Uncle Hawk who was scraping dishes while my mother cleared the table. They were silent a moment. Then my mother said, "Who in the world could it be, Uncle Hawk?" and he said "I wonder myself." I said, "Well, hurry. It is a stranger and the screen door is not even locked." He did not hurry. My mother and I stood and watched him get ready—washing with the Castile soap he keeps for his fine long hands tough as shark hide, adjusting suspenders, the garters on his sleeves, inspecting his shoes. Towards the end I looked at my mother in anxiety. She winked at me and said, "Go on, Uncle Hawk. It certainly is not Jesus *yet*." Not smiling he said, "I wish it was" and went. Again I looked to my mother and again she winked and beckoned me behind her into the hall where we could watch the door and the meeting. Uncle Hawk said "Good evening" but did not bow, and the man said, "Are you Hawk Reid?" Then he mumbled something about life insurance— did Uncle Hawk have enough life, fire, burial insurance? Uncle Hawk said, "My life is not worth paying on every week. I do not have nothing to insure for fire but a pocketknife and it is iron, and Mr. Jeff McCraw is burying me." The man mumbled some more. Uncle Hawk said "No" and the man reached for the handle to the screen that separated them. Uncle Hawk reached to lock the screen but too slow, and there was the man on us, two feet from Hawk, fifteen from my mother and me. Hawk said, "Nobody asked you to come in here" and drew back his arm (nearly eighty years old) to strike. My mother and I had not made a sound, and I had mostly watched her not the door as she was grinning but then she laughed. Uncle Hawk turned on her, his arm still coiled, then back to the man who was looking up now not moving, and then Hawk laughed, doubled over helpless. The man walked in right past him slowly and stopped six feet from me, holding out his hand to take—he and I the two in the room not laughing. So I knew he had come for me, that I was his and would have to go. His hand stayed out in the glove towards me. There were three lines of careful black stitching down the back of the pale gray leather, the kind of gloves I wanted that are not made for boys. Still I could not take his hand just then, and not for terror. I was really not afraid but suddenly sorry to leave people who had been good to me, the house which I knew. That was what locked me there. I must have stood half a minute that way, and I must have looked worse and worse because my mother said, "Look at his eyes" and pointed me towards the man's face. I looked and at once they were what they had been all along—Jeff McCraw's eyes, the size and color of used nickles, gentle beyond disguising. I said to him then fast and high, "I thought you were my real father and had come to get me." He took off his derby and the old glasses and said, "I *am*, Preacher. I *have*, Preacher," and I ran to circle his thighs with my arms, to hide my tears in the hollow beneath the black overcoat. And I did hide them. When I looked up, everybody thought I had loved the joke like them. But I had not. I had loved my father found at the end with his

hand stretched out. But I hoped not to find him again
that way under glasses and powder, mumbling; so when
he came into my bedroom to kiss me that night, I asked
would he do me a favor. He said, "What?" and I said,
"Please warn me before you dress up ever again." He
said he would and then my mother walked in and hearing us said, "You will not need warning. Just stare at his
eyes first thing. He cannot hide those." But he always
warns me as he promised he would—except at
Christmas when he comes in a cheap flannel suit and
rayon beard that any baby could see is false—and even
though I know in advance that on a certain evening he
will arrive as a tramp to scare my Aunt Lola or as a tax
collector or a man from the farm office to tell my Uncle
Paul he has planted illegal tobacco and must plow it
under or suffer, still I fasten on his eyes and hold to them
till somebody laughs and he finds time to wink at me.

As I fasten on them now heading home. He travels
of course as himself tonight in a brown vested suit and
a solid green tie so I see him plain—what is clear in
dashboard light—and though I love him, though I rest
in his hollow lap now happier than any other place, I
know he cannot be my hero. And I list the reasons to
myself. Heroes are generally made by war. My father
was born in 1900 so the nearest he got to the First
World War was the National Guard and in October
1918 an Army camp near Morehead City, N.C. where
he spent six weeks in a very wrinkled uniform (my
mother has his picture) till peace arrived, so desper-
ately homesick that he saved through the whole six
weeks the bones of a chicken lunch his mother gave
him on leaving home. And when I woke him a year
ago from his Sunday nap to ask what was Pearl Harbor

that the radio was suddenly full of, he was well and young enough to sign for the Draft and be nervous but too old to serve. He does own two guns—for protection an Army .45 that his brother brought him from France, never wanting to see it again, and for hunting a double-barreled shotgun with cracked stock—but far as I know he has never shot anything but himself (that time he was a boy) and two or three dozen wharf rats, rabbits and squirrels. Nor is he even in his quiet life what heroes generally must be—physically brave. Not that chances often arise for that class of bravery. I had not seen him face any ordeal worse than a flat tire till a while ago when we had our first mock air raid in Randolph. He took an armband, helmet, blackjack and me, and we drove slowly to the power station which was his post and sat in the cold car thinking it would end soon, but it did not and I began to wonder was it real, were the Germans just beyond hearing, heading towards us? Then he opened his door and we slid out and stood on the hill with great power batteries singing behind us and looked down at the smothered town. I said, "What will we do if the Germans really come?" Not waiting he pointed towards what I guessed was Sunset Avenue (his sense of direction being good) and said, "We would high-tail it there to where your mother is liable to burn down the house any minute with all those candles." He did not laugh but the siren went and lights began and we headed home—the house stinking tallow on through the night and I awake in bed wondering should I tell him, "If you feel that way you ought to resign as warden"? deciding, "No, if Hitler comes let him have the power. What could we do anyhow, Father with a blackjack, me with nothing?

—hold off steel with our pitiful hands?" (the hand he
touches me with again now, his wounded hand but the
wrist so whole so full, under its curls so ropey I cannot
ring it, trying now I cannot capture it in my hand so I
trace one finger through its curls, tracing my name into
him as older boys gouge names, gouge love into trees,
into posts—gouge proudly. But with all the love I
mentioned before, I do not trace proudly. I know him
too well, know too many lacks, and my finger stops in
the rut where his pulse would be if I could ever find it
(I have tried, I cannot find it, maybe could not stand it
if I did). I shut my eyes not to see his face for fear he
will smile, and continue to name his lacks to myself.
He makes people wait—meaning me and my mother.
He is a salesman and travels, and sometimes when
school is out, I travel with him, hoping each time
things will go differently. They start well always (riding
and looking though never much talking) till we come
to the house where he hopes to sell a stove or refriger-
ator. We will stop in the yard. He will sit a minute,
looking for dangerous dogs, then reach for his briefcase, open his door and say, "Wait here, Preacher. I
will be straight back" and I will say "All right" and he
will turn back to me, "You do not mind that, do you,
darling?"—"Not if you remember I am out here and
do not spend the day." He of course says he will remember and goes, but before he has gone ten yards I
can see that memory rise through his straw hat like
steam, and by the time a woman says, "Step in the
house," I am out of his mind as if I was part of the car
that welcomed this chance to cool and rest. Nothing
cool about it (being always summer when I travel with
him), and I sit and sweat, shooing out flies and freez-

ing if a yellowjacket comes, and when twenty minutes has gone by the clock, I begin to think, "If this was all the time he meant to give me, why did he bring me along?" And that rushes on into, "Why did he get me, why did he want me at all if he meant to treat me the way he does, giving me as much time each day as it takes to kiss me goodbye when I go to school and again at night in case we die in each other's absence?" And soon I am rushing through ways he neglects me daily. He will not for instance *teach* me. Last fall I ordered an axe from Sears and Roebuck with my own money, asking nobody's permission, and when it came —so beautiful—he acted as if I had ordered mustard gas and finally said I could keep it if I promised not to use it till he showed me the right way. I promised— and kept my promise—and until this day that axe has done nothing but wait on my wall, being taken down every night, having its lovely handle stroked, its dulling edge felt fearfully. And baseball. He has told me how he played baseball when he was my age, making it sound the happiest he ever was, but he cannot make me catch a fly-ball. I have asked him for help, and he went so far as to buy me a glove and spend half an hour in the yard throwing at me, saying "Like this, Preacher" when I threw at him, but when I failed to stop ball after ball, he finally stopped trying and went in the house, not angry or even impatient but never again offering to teach me what he loved when he was my age, what had won him friends. Maybe he thought he was being kind. Maybe he thought he had shamed me, letting me show him my failure. He had, he had. But if he knew how furious I pray when I am the outfield at school recess (pray that flies go any way but

mine), how struck, how shrunk, how abandoned I feel
when prayer fails and a ball splits hot through my
hopeless hand to lie daring me to take it and throw it
right while some loud boy no bigger than I, no better
made, trots a free home run—he would try again, do
nothing but try. Or maybe there just come stretches
when he does not care, when he does not love me or
want me in his mind much less his sight—scrambling
on the ground like a hungry fice for a white leather
ball any third-grade girl could catch, sucking his life,
his time, his fun for the food I need, the silly clothes,
sucking the joy out of what few hopes he may have
seen when his eyes were shut ten years ago, when he
and my mother made me late in the night—that is the
stuff he makes me think when he goes and leaves me
stuck in the car, stuck for an hour many times so that
finally sunk in desperation I begin to know he is sick in
there—that his heart has seized as he knows it will or
that strange woman is wild and has killed him silent
with a knife, with poison, or that he has sold his stove
and said goodbye and gone out the back in secret
across a field into pines to leave us forever, to change
his life. And I will say to myself, "You have got to
move—run to the road and flag a car and go for the
sheriff," but the house door will open and he will be
there alive still grinning, then calming his face in the
walk through the yard, wiping his forehead, smiling
when he sees me again, when he recollects he has a
son and I am it (am one anyhow, the one old enough to
follow him places and wait). Before I can swallow what
has jammed my throat, my heart in the previous hour,
he will have us rolling—the cool breeze started and
shortly his amends, my reward for waiting. It is always

the same, his amends. It is stories about him being my age, especially about his father—Charles McCraw, "Cupe" McCraw who was clerk to the Copeland Register of Deeds, raised six children which were what he left (and a house, a wife, several dozen jokes) when he died sometime before I was born—and he needs no crutch to enter his stories such as "Have I told you this?" He knows he has told me, knows I want it again every time he can spare. He will light a cigarette with a safety match (he threw away the car's lighter long ago out the window down an embankment, thinking *it* was a match) and then say, "No sir. If I live to be ninety, I never want to swallow another cigarette." That is the first of the story about him at my age being sent outdoors by his father to shut off the water when a hard freeze threatened. The valve was sunk in the ground behind the house, and he was squatting over it cursing because it was stiff and pulling on the cigarette he had lit to warm him—when he looked in the frozen grass by his hand and there were black shoes and the ends of trousers. He did not need to look further. It was his father so while he gave one last great turn to the valve, he flipped his lower lip out and up (and here at age forty-two he imitates the flip, swift but credible) and swallowed the cigarette, fire included. Then he may say, "How is your bladder holding out, Preacher? Do you want to run yonder into those bushes?" I will say "No" since I cannot leak in open air, and he will say, "Father had a colored boy named Peter who worked round the house. *Peee-ter*, Peter called it. The first day we had a telephone connected, Father called home from the courthouse to test it. I was home from school —supposed to be sick—and I answered. He did not catch my voice so he said 'Who is this?' I said '*Pee-ter*,' and he thought he would joke a little. He said 'Peter *who*?' I said 'Mr. *McCraw's* Peee-ter,' and he said, 'Hang up, fool, and don't ever answer that thing again!' I waited for him to come home that evening, and he finally came with a box of Grapenuts for me, but he did not mention Peter or the telephone so I didn't either, never mentioned it till the day he died. He died at night . . ."

But *tonight*. This hard winter night in 1942 and he is silent—my father—his eyes on darkness and road to get me safely home as if I was cherished, while I rush on behind shut eyes through all that last—his size, his lacks, his distances—still threading my finger through curls of his wrist, a grander wrist then he needs or deserves. I find his pulse. It rises sudden to my winnowing finger, waylays, appalls, *traps* it. I ride his life with the pad of flesh on my middle finger, and it heaves against me steady and calm as if it did not know I ruled its flow, that poor as I am at games and play, I could press in now, press lightly first so he would not notice, then in and in till his foot would slack on the gas, his head sink heavy to his chest, his eyes shut on me (on what I cause), the car roll still and I be left with what I have made—his permanent death. Towards that picture, that chance, my own pulse rises untouched, unwanted—grunting aloud in the damp stripes under my groins, the tender sides of my windpipe, sides of my heels, the pad of my sinking finger. My finger coils to my side, my whole hand clenches, my eyes clamp tighter, but—innocently surely—he speaks for the first time since begging my pardon. "Am I dying, Preacher?"

I look up at him. "No sir. What do you mean?"

"I mean you left my pulse like a bat out of Hell. I wondered did you feel bad news?"

"No sir, it is going fine. I just never felt it before, and it gave me chills." He smiles at the road and we slide on a mile or more till I say, "Are you *scared* of dying?"

He keeps me waiting so I look past him through glass to the sky for a distant point to anchor on—the moon, a planet, Betelgeuse. Nothing is there. All is drowned under cloud but I narrow my eyes and strain to pierce the screen. Then when I am no longer waiting, he says, "It is the main thing I am scared of."

I come back to him. "Everybody is going to die."

"So they tell me. So they tell me. But that is one crowd I would miss if I could. Gladly."

I am not really thinking. "What do people mean when they say somebody is their personal hero?"

It comes sooner than I expect. "Your hero is what you need to be."

"Then is Jesus your hero?"

"Why do you think that?"

"You say you are scared of dying. Jesus is the one that did not die."

He does not take it as funny which is right, and being no Bible scholar he does not name me the others that live on—Enoch, Elijah. I name them to myself but not to him. I have seen my chance. I am aiming now at discovery, and I strike inwards like Balboa mean and brave, not knowing where I go or will end or if I can live with what I find. But the next move is his. He must see me off. And he does. He tells me, "I think your hero has to be a man. Was Jesus a man?"

"No sir. He was God disguised."

"Well, that is it, you see. You would not stand a chance of being God—need to or not—so you pick somebody you have got half a chance of measuring up to."

In all my seeking I have not asked him. I ask him now. "Have you got a hero?"

Again he makes me wait and I *wait*. I look nowhere but at him. I do not think. Then he says, "Yes, I guess I do. But I never called it that to myself."

"What did you call it?"

"I didn't call it nothing. I was too busy trying to get through alive."

"Sir?"

"—Get through some trouble I had. I *had* some troubles and when I did there was generally a person I could visit and talk to till I eased. Then when I left him and the trouble came back, I would press down on *him* in my mind—something he told me or how he shook my hand goodbye. Sometimes that tided me over. Sometimes."

He has still not offered a name. To help him I hold out the first one at hand. "Is it Dr. Truett?" (That is where we are coming from now tonight—a sermon in Raleigh by George W. Truett from Texas.)

The offer is good enough to make him think. (I know how much he admires Dr. Truett. He has one of his books and a sermon on records—"The Need for Encouragement"—that he plays two or three nights a year, standing in the midst of the room, giving what wide curved gestures seem right when Dr. Truett says for instance, " 'Yet now be strong, O Zerubbabel, saith the Lord; and be strong O Joshua, son of Josedech,

the high priest; and be strong, all ye people of the
land, saith the Lord, and work: for I am with you,
saith the Lord of hosts: according to the word that I
covenanted with you when ye came out of Egypt, so
my spirit remaineth among you: fear ye not.'" And
here we have come this long way to see him in January
with snow due to fall by morning.) But he says—my
father, "No, not really. Still you are close." Then a
wait—"You are warm."

"Does that mean it is a preacher?"

"Yes."

"Mr. Barden?"

"I guess he is it."

I knew he was—or would have known if I had
thought—but I do not know why. He is nothing but
the Baptist minister in Copeland, my father's home—
half a head shorter than Father, twenty years older,
light and dry as kindling with flat bands of gray hair,
white skin the day shines through if he stands by windows, Chinese eyes, bird ankles, a long voice for saying things such as "Jeff, I am happy to slide my legs
under the same table with yours" and poor digestion
(he said that last the one day he ate with us; my
mother had cooked all morning, and he ate a cup of
warm milk)—but he is one of the people my father
loves, one my mother is jealous of, and whenever we
visit Copeland (we left there when I was two), there
will come a point after dinner on Sunday when my
father will stand and without speaking start for the car.
If it is winter he may get away unseen, but in summer
everybody will be on the porch, and Junie will say,
"Jeff is headed to save Brother Barden's soul." My
mother will laugh. My father will smile and nod but go

and be gone till evening and feel no need to explain when he returns, only grin and agree to people's jokes.

But *tonight*, has he not just offered to explain? and to me who have never asked? So I ask, "Mr. Barden is so skinny. What has he got that you need to be?"

"Before you were born he used to be a lot of things. Still is."

All this time he has not needed his hand on the wheel. It has stayed heavy on me. I slip my hand towards it. I test with my finger, tapping. He turns his palm and takes me, gives me the right to say "Name some things." I fear if he looks at me, we will go back silent (he has not looked down since we started with his pulse), and I roll my face deep into his side, not to take his eyes. But they do not come. He does not look. He does not press my hand in his, and the load of his wrist even lightens. I think it will leave but it lifts a little and settles further on like a folded shield over where I am warmest, takes up guard, and then he is talking the way he must, the best he can, to everything but me—the glass, the hood, the hoop of light we push towards home.

"I have done things you would not believe—and will not believe when you get old enough to do them yourself. I have come home at night where your mother was waiting and said things to her that were worse than a beating, then gone again and left her still waiting till morning, till sometimes night again. And did them knowing I would not do them to a dog. Did them drunk and wild, knowing she loved me and would not leave me even though her sisters said, 'Leave him. He won't change now,' would not even raise her voice. O Preacher, it was Hell. We were both

in Hell with the lid screwed down, not a dollar between us except what I borrowed—from Negroes
sometimes when friends ran out—to buy my liquor to
keep me wild. You were not born yet, were not
thought of, God knows not wanted the way I was
going. It was 1930. I was thirty years old and my life
looked over, and I didn't know why or whether I
wanted it different, but here came Mr. Barden skinny
as you say, just sitting by me when I could sit still,
talking when I could listen, saying 'Hold up, Jeff.
Promise God something before you *die*.' But Preacher,
I didn't. I drank up two more years, driving thousands
of miles on mirey roads in a model-A Ford to sell little
scraps of life insurance to wiped-out farmers that did
not have a pot to pee in, giving your mother a dollar or
so to buy liver with on a Saturday or a pound of ho-
miny I could not swallow. And then that spring when
the bottom looked close, I slipped and started you on
the way. When I knew you were coming—Preacher,
for days I was out of what mind I had left myself. I do
not know what I did but I *did* things, and finally when
I had run some sort of course, your mother sent for
Mr. Barden and they got me still. He said, 'Jeff, I
cherish you, mean as you are. But what can I do if you
go on murdering yourself, tormenting your wife?' I
told him, 'You can ask the Lord to stop that baby.' I
told him that. But you came on every day *every day*
like a tumor till late January and she hollered to me
you were nearly here. But you were not. You held
back twenty-four hours as if you knew who was waiting
outside, and Dr. Haskins told me—after he had struggled with your mother all day, all night—'Jeff, one of
your family is going to die but I don't know which.' I

said, 'Let it be me' and he said he wished he could. I went outdoors to Paul's woodshed and told Jesus, 'If you take Rhew or take that baby, then take me too. But if You can, save her and save that baby, and I make You this promise—I will change my life.' I asked Him, 'Change my life.' So He saved you two and I started trying to change my life, am trying right now God knows. Well, Mr. Barden has helped me out every once in a while—talking to me or just sitting calm, showing me his good heart. Which, Preacher, I need."

I can tell by his voice he is not through, but he stops, leaving raw quiet like a hole beneath us. I feel that because I have stayed awake, and my finger slips to the trough of his wrist where the pulse was before. It is there again awful. I take it, count it long as I can and say, "It feels all right to me, sir" (not knowing of course how right would feel). He says he is glad which frees me to see Mr. Barden again. I call up his face and pick it for anything new. At first it is very much the same—bloodless, old—but I settle on the faded stripes of his lips and strain to picture them years ago saying the things that were just now reported. They move, speak and for a moment I manage to see his face as a wedge—but aimed elsewhere, making no offer to split me clean from my lacks *my* foes. So I let it die and I say to my father, "I still think Jesus is your real hero."

Glad for his rest, he is ready again. "Maybe so. Maybe so. But Mr. Barden was what I could *see*."

"Who has seen Jesus?"

"Since He died, you mean?"

"Yes sir."

"Several, I guess. Dr. Truett for one."

I know the story—it is why I have come this far to hear an old man tremble for an hour—but I request it again.

"Well, as I understand it, years ago when he was young, he asked a friend to come hunting with him. He came and they went in the woods together, and after a while he shot his friend. By accident but that didn't make him feel any better. He knew some people would always say he killed the man on purpose."

"Maybe he did."

"No he didn't. Hold on."

"How do you know?"

"The same way *he* knew—because after he sweated drops of blood in misery, Jesus came to him one evening in a dream and said not to grieve any more but to live his life and do what he could."

"Does that mean he really saw Jesus?—seeing Him in his sleep?"

"How else could you see Him since He is dead so long?"

I tell him the chance that is one of my hopes, my terrors—"He could walk in your house in daylight. Then you could step around Him. You could put out your hand and He would be there. But in just a dream how would you know? What would keep Him from being a trick?"

"The way He would look. His face, His hands."

"The scars, you mean?"

"They would help. But no—" This is hard for him. He stops and thinks for fully a mile. "I mean whether or not He had the face to say things such as 'Be ye perfect as God is perfect'—not even say '*try* to be,' just '*be*'—a face that could change people's lives."

"People do not *know* what He looks like, Father.
That is half the trouble." We are now on one of our
oldest subjects. We started three years ago when I first
went to vacation Bible school. At the end of that two
weeks after we had made our flour-paste model of a
Hebrew water hole, they gave us diplomas that were
folded leaflets with our name inside and a golden star
but on the cover their idea of Jesus—set by a palm
under light such as comes after storms (blurred, with
piece of a rainbow) and huddled around Him, one
each of the earth's children in native dress, two or
three inside His arms but all aiming smiles at His face
(jellied eyes, tan silk beard, clean silk hair, pink lips
that could not call a dog to heel much less children or
say to His mother, "Who is my mother?" and call her
"Woman" from the bitter cross). I took the picture but
at home that night I handed it to my father and asked
if he thought that face was possible? He looked and
said it was one man's guess, not to worry about it, but I
did and later after I had studied picture Bibles and
Christ and the Fine Arts by Cynthia Pearl Maus full of
hairy Jesuses by Germans mostly—Clementz, Dei-
trich, Hofmann, Lang, Plockhorst, Von Uhde, Wehle
—I asked him if in all the guessers, there was one who
knew? any Jesus to count on? He said he thought there
was but in Student's Bibles, the ones they give to boys
studying ministry. I said had he seen one? He had not
and I asked if he could buy me one or borrow Mr.
Barden's for me to trace? He said he did not think so,
that Student's Bibles were confidential, secrets for
good men.

So tonight I ask him, "Then how did he look in your

mind when I was being born and Mother was dying?"

"He didn't look nohow *that* day. I was not seeing faces. I was doing business. If I saw anything it was rocks underfoot, those smooth little rocks Paul hauled from the creek to spread in his yard."

"I think it is awful."

"What?"

"Him not appearing. Why did Dr. Truett see Him and you could not?"

"Maybe he needed to worse than me. He had killed a man, killed somebody else. I was just killing me, making others watch me do it."

"That is no reason."

"Preacher, if I was as good a man as George W. Truett—half the man—I would be seeing Jesus every day or so, be *fishing* with Him."

"I am not joking, Father. It is awful, I think—Him not helping you better than that."

"Preacher, I didn't mind"—which even with this night's new information is more or less where we always end. It does not worry my father that he is not privileged to see the secret. But it scalds, torments any day of mine in which I think that the face with power to change my life is hid from me and reserved for men who have won their fight—(when He Himself claimed He sought the lost), will always be hid, leaving me to work dark. As my father has done, does, must do— not minding, just turning on himself his foe with nothing for hero but Mr. Barden when it could have been Jesus if He had appeared, His gouged hands, His real face, the one He deserved that changes men.

We are quiet again, so quiet I notice the sound of the engine. I have not heard it tonight before. It bores through the floor, crowds my ears, and turning my eyes I take the mileage—sixty-three thousand to round it off. My father travels to his work as I say, and this Pontiac has borne him three times around the earth—the equal of that nearly. It will get us home together, alive, and since in a heavy rush I am tired, I sleep where I am, in his heat, in his hollow. Of course I do not think I am sleeping. I dream I am awake, that I stand on the near side of sleep and yearn, but it *is* a dream and as sudden again I wake—my head laid flat on the mohair seat, blood gathered hot in my eyes that stare up at nothing. My head lifts a little (stiff on my neck), my eyes jerk round collecting terror—the motor runs gentle, the knob of the heater burns red, burns warm, but the car is still and my father is gone. Where he was the dashboard light strikes empty nothing. My head falls back and still half dreaming I think, "They have won at last. They have caught us, come between us. We have ended apart." I say that last aloud and it wakes me fully so I lie on (my head where his loaded lap should be) and think what seems nearer truth—"He has left as I always knew he would to take up his life in secret." Then I plunge towards the heart of my fear—"He knew just now what I thought when I pressed his pulse, and he could not bear my sight any more." Then deeper towards the heart—"God has taken him from me as punishment for causing his death just now in my mind. But why did He not take me?" Still He did not. I am left. So I rise and strain to see out the glass, to know my purpose for being here, what trials lie between me and morning, what vengeance. The first is snow. The headlights shine and in their outward upward hoop there is only flat gobs of snow that saunter into frozen grass and survive. The grass of the shoulder is all but smothered, the weeds of the bank already bent, meaning I have slept long enough for my life to wreck beyond hope—my father vanished and I sealed in a black Pontiac with stiff death held back only long as the draining battery lasts and now too late, no hero to turn to. My forehead presses into the dark windshield. For all the heater's work, the cold crawls in through glass, through flesh, through skull to my blood, my brain.

So I pray. My eyes clamped now, still pressed to the glass, knowing I have not prayed for many weeks past (with things going well), I swallow my shame and naked in fear ask, "Send me my father. Send me help. If You help me now, if You save my life, I will change —be brave, be free with my gifts. Send somebody good." My eyes click open on answered prayer—coming slow from the far edge of light a tall man hunched, his face to the ground hid, head wrapped in black, a black robe bound close about him, his arms inside, bearing towards me borne on the snow as if on water leaving no tracks, his shadow crouched on the snow like a following bird, giant, black (killing? kind?). I stay at the glass, further prayer locked in my throat, waiting only for the sign of my fate. Then the robe spreads open. The man's broad hands are clasped on his heart, turned inward, dark. It is Jesus I see, Jesus I shall touch moments from now—shall lift His face, probe His wounds, kiss His eyes. He is five steps away. I slip from the glass, fall back on my haunches, turn to the driver's door where He already stands, say silent, "If Father could not see Your face, why must I?"—say to the opening door "Thank You, Sir," close my lips to take His unknown kiss.

He says, "Excuse me leaving you asleep," and it is my father come back disguised. "I had to go pee—down that hill in the snow." (He points down the road as if he had covered miles not feet.) "I thought you were dead to the world."

I say, "I *was*"—I laugh—"and I thought you were Jesus, that you had been taken and I was left and Jesus was coming to claim me. I was about to *see* Him."

Standing outside, the warm air rushing towards him, he shrugs the coat from his shoulders, lifts the scarf from his head, lays them in back, slides onto the seat. Shrinking from cold I have crawled almost to the opposite door, but kneeling towards him. He faces me and says, "I am sorry to disappoint you, Preacher."

I say "Yes sir" and notice he smiles very slow, very deep from his eyes—but ahead at the road. Then he says I had better lie down. I crawl the two steps and lie as before, and we move on so I have no chance to return his smile, to show I share his pleasure. Still I root my head deep in his lap and hope for a chance before sleep returns. The chance never comes. Snow occupies his eyes, his hands. He cannot face me again or test for warmth. Even his mind is surely on nothing but safety. Yet his face is new. Some scraps of the beauty I planned for Jesus hang there—on the corners of his mouth serious now, beneath his glasses in eyes that are no longer simply kind and gray but have darkened and burn new power far back and steady (the power to stop in his tracks and *turn*), on his ears still purple with cold but flared against danger like perfect ugly shells of blind sea life, on his wrists I cannot ring with my hand, stretched from white cuffs at peace on the wheel but shifting with strength beyond soldier's, beyond slave's—and I think, "I will look till I know my father, till all this new disguise falls away leaving him clear as before." I look but his face shows no sign of retreat, and still as he is and distant, it is hard to stare, painful then numbing. I feel sleep rise from my feet like blood. When it reaches my head I shut my eyes to flush it back, but it surges again and I know I have lost. My own hands are free—he has not touched me, cannot—so my right hand slips to the gap in my pants, cups itself warm on warmer trinkets long since asleep, soft with blood like new birds nested drowsy. I follow them into darkness, thinking on the threshold, "Now I have lost all hope of knowing my father's life," cupping closer, warmer this hand as I sink.

First in my dream I am only this hand yet have eyes to see—but only this hand and a circle of light around it. It is larger by half than tonight, and black stubble has sprung to shade its back, its new thick veins, its gristly cords showing plain because his hand is cupped too, round like a mold, hiding what it makes. It lifts. What it has molded are the kernels, the knobs of a man still twice the size of mine I held before I slept, but cold, shrunk and shrinking as my hand lifts—their little life pouring out blue through veins gorged like sewers that tunnel and vanish under short lank hairs, grizzled. Then I have ears. I hear the blood rustle like silk as it leaves, retreats, *abandons*, and my hand shuts down, clamps on the blood to turn its race, to warm again, fill again what I hold. But the rustle continues not muffled, and my hand presses harder, squeezes the kernels. Through my fingers green piss streams cold,

corrosive. But my hand is locked. It cannot move. I
am bound to what I have made, have caused, and seeing only this terror, I find a voice to say, "If I cannot
leave may I see what I do?" The light swells in a hoop
from my hand filling dimly a room and in that room
my whole body standing by a bed—the body I will
have as a man—my hand at the core of a man's
stripped body laid yellow on the narrow bed. Yet with
this new light my original eyes have stayed where they
started—on my crushing hand and beneath it. I tear
them left to see the rest. So I start at his feet raised
parallel now but the soles pressed flat by years of
weight, the rims of the heels and the crowded toes
guarded by clear callus, the veins of the insteps
branching toward shins like blades of antique war polished deadly, marred by sparse hair, the knees like
grips to the blades, the thighs ditched inward to what I
crush—his hollow his core that streams on thin with
no native force but sure as if drained by magnets in the
earth. Then his hands at his sides clenched but the little fingers separate, crouched, gathering ridges in the
sheet. Then his firm belly drilled deep by the navel, his
chest like the hull of a stranded boat, shaved raw, violet paps sunk and from under his left armpit a line
traced carefully down his side, curved under his ribs,
climbing to the midst of his breast—the letter J perfect, black, cut into him hopeless to dredge out a lung,
laced with gut stiff as wire. Then under a tent of soft
wrinkled glass his face which of course is my father's—
the face he will have when I am this man—turned
from me, eyes shut, lips shut, locked in the monstrous
stillness of his rest. So he does not watch me, shows no
sign of the pain I must cause. Yet I try again to lift my

fingers, to set him free, but rocking the heel of my hand, I see our skin has joined maybe past parting. I struggle though—gentle to spare his rest. I step back slowly, hoping this natural movement will peel us clean, but what I have pressed comes with me as if I had given love not pain. I speak again silent to whoever gave me light just now, say, "Set him free. Let me leave him whole in peace." But that prayer fails and turning my eyes I pull against him, ready to wound us both if I must. Our joint holds fast but the rustle beneath my hand swells to scraping, to high short grunts. "Jesus," I say—I speak aloud—"Come again. Come now. I do not ask to see Your face but come in *some* shape now." A shudder begins beneath my hand in his core our core that floods through his belly, his breast to his throat, bearing with it the noise that dims as it enters the tent. I stare through the glass. His head rolls towards me, his yellow lips split to release the noise, his eyes slide open on a quarter-inch of white. The noise scrapes on but behind the tent it is not words—is it rage or pain or wish, is it meant for me? With my free left hand I reach for the tent to throw it back, saying, "Stop. Stop," but I cannot reach so "Father," I say, "I beg your pardon. Pardon me this, I will change my life—will turn in my tracks on myself my foe with you as shield." But he yields no signal. The eyes shut again, the lips shut down on the noise, the shudder runs out as it came, to our core. What my free hand can reach it touches—his wrist. What pulse was there is stopped, and cold succeeds it till with both hands I press hard ice, final as any trapped in the Pole. I can see clearer now, my terror calmed by his grander terror, the peace of his wounds, and facing his abandoned face I say again (to the place, the dream), "Pardon me this, I will change my life. I make this . . ." But pardon comes to stop my speech. My cold hands lift from his hollow, his wrist. My own hot life pours back to claim them. Then those hands fail, those eyes, my dream. A shift of my headrest lifts me from sleep.

I face my live father's present body—my present eyes on his belly but *him*, *tonight*, above me, around me, shifting beneath me. My lips are still open, a trail of spit snails down my cheek, my throat still holds the end of my dream, "I make this promise." So my first thought is fear. Have I spoken aloud what I watched in my dream? Have I warned my father of his waiting death? offered my promise, my life too early? I roll away from his belt to see—and see I am safe. He is what he has been before tonight, been all my life, unchanged by my awful news, my knowledge, undisguised—his ears, his cheeks flushed with healthy blood that also throbs in the broad undersides of his wrists on the wheel, in the wounded fat of his hand, his hollow, even in his eyes which are still ahead on the road for safety, able, unblinking but calm and light as if through snow he watched boys playing skillful games with natural grace.

His legs shift often under me now—braking, turning, accelerating—and we move forward slowly past regular street lamps that soar through the rim of my sight, gold at the ends of green arms. We are in some town. From its lamps, its wires, its hidden sky, I cannot say which—but not home yet I trust, I hope. I am not prepared for home and my mother, the rooms that surround my swelling lacks, direct sight of my doomed father. I need silent time to hoard my secret out of my face deep into my mind, granting my father twelve years fearless to work at his promise, freeing myself to gather in private the strength I will need for my own promise the night he dies, my own first turn on what giant foes I will have as a man. And clamping my eyes I seize my dream and thrust it inward, watching it suck down a blackening funnel, longing to follow it. But his legs shift again, his arms swing left, our wheels strike gravel, stop. Beyond the glass in our stationary light are bare maple limbs accepting snow, limbs of the one tree I climb with ease. Too sudden we are home and my father expels in a seamless shudder the care, the attention that bound him these last three hours. His legs tense once, gather to spring from beneath my weight, then subside, soften. I ride the final surge, then face him—smiling as if just startled from sleep.

He takes my smile, stores it as a gift. "Did you sleep well, Preacher?"

I hunch my shoulders, say "Thank you, sir," and behind my lie floods sudden need—to rise, board him, cherish with my hands, my arms while there still is time this huge gentle body I know like my own, which made my own (made half anyhow) and has hurt nobody since the day I was born.

But he says, "Lift up. Look yonder at the door."

I roll to my knees. Through glass and snow, behind small panes, white curtains, in the center of the house no longer ours stands my mother in a flannel robe, hand raised in welcome the shape of fire. "She waited," I say.

"She waited," he says and reaches for his scarf, his coat, beckons me to him, drapes them around me, steps to the white ground and turning, offers me open arms. Kneeling I ask him, "What do you mean?"

"I mean to save your life, to carry you over this snow."

"Heavy as *I* am?—you and *your* heart?"

But he says no more. His mind is made, his trip is ended. He is nearly home, facing rest, accepting snow like the trees while I stall. Then he claps his palms one time, and I go on my knees out of dry car heat through momentary snow into arms that circle, enfold me, lift me, bear me these last steps home over ice—my legs hung bare down his cooling side, face to his heart, eyes blind again, mind folding in me for years to come his literal death and my own swelling foes, lips against rough brown wool saying to myself as we rise to the porch, to my waiting mother (silent, in the voice I will have as a man), "They did not separate us tonight. We finished alive, together, whole. This one more time."

ABOUT THE AUTHOR

Born in Macon, North Carolina, in 1933, Reynolds Price attended North Carolina schools and received his Bachelor of Arts degree from Duke University. As a Rhodes Scholar he studied for three years at Merton College, Oxford, receiving the Bachelor of Letters with a thesis on Milton. In 1958 he returned to Duke, where he is now James B. Duke Professor of English. His first novel A LONG AND HAPPY LIFE appeared in 1962. It was followed by a volume of stories, THE NAMES AND FACES OF HEROES; A GENEROUS MAN (a novel); LOVE AND WORK (a novel); PERMANENT ERRORS (stories); THINGS THEMSELVES (essays and scenes); THE SURFACE OF EARTH (a novel); EARLY DARK (a play); A PALPABLE GOD (translations from the Bible with an essay on the origins and life of narrative); THE SOURCE OF LIGHT (a novel); VITAL PROVISIONS (poems); PRIVATE CONTENTMENT (a play); KATE VAIDEN (a novel); THE LAWS OF ICE (poems); A COMMON ROOM: ESSAYS 1954-1987; GOOD HEARTS (a novel); and CLEAR PICTURES (a memoir).

THE CELEBRATED AUTHOR

REYNOLDS PRICE